Pride & Dignity

Pride & Dignity

The saga of Cheno Cortinas

HOLON
PUBLISHING

Pride & Dignity
Copyright © 2013 by Rodolfo J. Walss

Art by Rodolfo J. Walss

Published by Holon Publishing
& Collective Press

ISBN-978-0-9853027-2-6

www.holonpublishing.com

4001 East 3rd Street Bloomington IN,
47408

Publisher's Review
Pride & Dignity

Upon my initial review of the manuscript for Pride & Dignity, I was immediately greeted with intensity and cinematic glory; I had entered the set of a film noir with Spanish guitars vibrantly racing and gunfire violently blazing. I had to savor each chapter of this tale as though I were sipping a most delicate wine in the sunset of some exotic land far from my own.

Yet not far, for as this literary epic, set during the Mexican-American war of the 19th century, reads vibrantly like our favorite blockbuster classics, it reminds us clearly of our own time, when governments are all-too concerned with where their borders are drawn. Between nations, and between hearts, these borders divide only in false pride; for we see clearly in this excellent tale of fire, passion, love and betrayal, that our worlds are reflections of each other, across borders and without boundaries.

Close to my heart, Pride & Dignity is filled with poetic nuance and lavish juxtapositions of gorgeous landscapes, sunsets and musical semblances of nature's beauty with the bloodshed and warfare of forging nations fighting for supremacy in a new and growing world.

We are taken on the journey of Juan Nepomuceno Cortina Goseascochea, or Cheno Cortinas, who is loved and adored by his people and feared with fervor by the American aristocrats who seek to subvert his people and make them as slaves in their own lands. But feared with much alack, for Cheno Cortinas is a noble, honest and fair man, though endowed with abundance from his life's exploits in trade. His compassion becomes the beacon of the tale's glory, for he strives intently to care for both his people of Mexico, and the Americans who live on his lands, in spite of the mounting tension between the growing nations. Apart from of his regal manner and splendor, we see elegantly captured that our protagonist is a man whose happiness is forged in simple pleasures, by the love of his fiancé Rafaela and his sweet surrender to the presence of nature in our beautiful world. But in spite of this man's humility and internal simplicity, he is no less a grandiose and romantic hero, who carries us on a wonderful journey with his friends and cohorts, Tomas, Chema, Sabas and many more who we grow to love (or disdain) as our tale progresses.

Without question, Pride & dignity is a thrilling read that will leave you wanting more to the very last page. It will make you laugh in its allegorical controversy, make you smile and cry with its sweetness, make your heart race with its passion, and ultimately give you chills with its beauty.

Jeremy Gotwals
Founder
Holon Publishing

CHAPTER 1

"Cheno, are you afraid?" said Jose Maria.

"A little," Cheno replied, as he wiped out the sweat from his forehead. "What about you, Chema?"

"I'm scared," he answered. "But, I don't recall ever seeing you afraid."

"That's because my biggest fear is being afraid, little brother. By the way, I'm proud that you have decided to join us in this fight. And let's not worry about Sabas, it's fine that he chose not to come along. Probably it's better that way. If tomorrow we die, someone will be there to look after Mama." Cheno slapped his cheek, drawing blood from the mosquito that had just stung him.

"Almost every vaquero from Matamoros to Camargo is with us in this fight," said Chema. "Since we were children, we have followed you. We chased and tamed wild horses and we kept the Comanche and the Apaches away from the ranchos. Although Sabas is the elder, he prefers staying home and taking care of the business side of the ranch. As you say, that's fine, some one ought to do it."

"He is a good man. You go to sleep now, little brother. I'll continue with the watch."

Cheno threw another log into the mesquite fire, got up and looked out into the darkness. Many more fires on the chaparral extended all the way to the Bahia. The close ones were friendly, but in the distance, he could see the many red and yellow dots from the American troops. The moist sea breeze made the late spring heat almost pleasant, but it could not overcome the strong odor of horses and horse dung that hung in the air. Cheno took a deep breath. This is my home, he thought. If they want it, they will have to feed its soil with their blood. He knew that coming from the coast there was only one route the invaders could go through to get to the river and Matamoros, and the mexicanos and tejanos were waiting for them. I'm sure General Arista has developed a good plan, he thought. We are ready. I'm ready. He walked to watch over the horses.

The sunrise was ablaze with the red, orange and yellow colors of the spring morning, the sharp tone of the trumpet started the movement of the men. Cheno mounted his colt and led his battalion of 60 young volunteers to the field. Many of them were his cousins from the ranchos along the river. They were to join the Tampico Battalion and the Lancers under General Anastasio Torrejon. There, they were to get in position to attack when ordered. The rising sun illuminated the moisture in the grasses and brightened everything. It hit Cheno's face almost directly. Jose Maria approached Cheno and looked at him admiringly.

"Cheno," he said, "if by the end of the day the soil is the same color as your beard, I hope that is mostly by their blood."

Cheno looked beyond the encampment to the battlefield. The green, brown, orange and golden grass was almost knee high. General Arista had positioned the cannons blocking the road. The infantry were ready to face the enemy. On the sides, by the mezquite and oaks, the cavalry got ready. Cheno and Jose Maria were along with them. He turned and looked to his brother. "We have fought the Karankawa and the Comanche, but this time is going to be different. Be valiant little brother, but above all ten cuidado and take good care of yourself."

Jose Maria - Chema to his family and friends - took off his broad hat, passed his hand over his long black hair, and looked up, his face brightening as he showed Cheno his white teeth. "Don't you worry brother; I'll be there by your side."

The sound of the trumpet alerted them. In the distance Cheno could see the Yankee line. Their infantry took positions, but they didn't seem ready to attack. It looked more like a defensive position. Then Cheno saw their cannons. He frowned. Those cannons were much smaller than any he had seen before, and they seemed not to have any problem in moving them around. They were mounted on light caissons and with the help of horses they could swing them around at will.

"What do you think?" Tomas Cabrera asked moving his horse alongside Cheno's.

Cheno turned and looked at his old friend, who appeared lees afraid than concerned. He noticed how his sun- tanned face had several dark spots, his eyes were bright and alert. A slender, strong vaquero who had been with the Cortina family as long as Cheno could remember. "They got better weapons, but that won't be enough. The Virgin of Guadalupe will give us the courage to protect the fatherland," answered Cheno as his nervous colt seemed to dance.

A blast announced the beginning of the battle. Both artilleries squared off with their best. With his heart pounding and his muscles tense, Cheno noticed how the Mexican blows fell short of their mark, while the Americans were painfully accurate. He felt pride then sorrow, seeing how the infantry held their lines in spite of the heavy impacts. The sound of the trumpet in the battalion called his attention.

"Men, the time has come," General Torrejon told them, "get in position. We ride against those cannons." Cheno could feel the tense muscles of his colt as he pulled on the reins. As soon as the order for attack was given, Cheno, along with all the volunteers and the Tampico battalion, burst into action. He gave his mount his head to proceed freely, his lance in the right hand pointing toward the enemy; he controlled his horse only by the strength of his legs. Knowing the terrain well, he guided his horse almost by intuition. They were one, a centaur on the move.

The thick, tall, razor-sharp grass cut his colt's legs, but the horse never wavered. The soil was uneven with the ruts of oxcarts and game trails, but thanks to the skill and the strength of his horse Cheno approached the enemy at a steady pace. His lance penetrated the flesh of an invader. He just let it go. Spinning his horse Cheno drew his revolver and fired at the soldiers who came running to protect the flank. Six shots, six enemies down. Tomas Cabrera, Jose Maria and most of the volunteers were by his side, but the rest of the cavalry had difficulty with the uneven and thicket soil. The enemy was able to re-position two of their cannons and was firing at the Tampico battalion at close range.

Cheno realized that they would have to retreat; Jose Maria and Tomas were surrounded by the enemy. Tomas' horse was taken down, felled by grape shot, and both were in serious trouble. Cheno went to their aid. Approaching Cabrera's outstretched hand, Cheno swung him on to the rear of his colt.

"Let's get out of here, little brother!" he yelled.

"Right," Chema yelled back.

Their horses jumped over the enemy lines and then galloped away feeling the buzzing of the enemy shots around them. Glancing back, Cheno saw that a heavy brush fire had started between the two opposing lines of cannons. Both sides ran to move the cannons and protect themselves from the fire. Dense smoke covered the retreat.

"Were you hurt?" Cheno asked Tomas and Jose Maria as soon as they were back to their original position.

"I think I have a wound in my back," said Tomas.

"I have some scratches. What about you, brother?" replied Jose Maria.

"Also just a few scratches. Let me take a look at your back, Tomas." Cheno examined Cabrera's back. "Nothing serious, old man. Mother still has a foreman." They all laughed.

They looked out on the battle field. The smoke had cleared. The relentless American artillery continued to pound the Mexican infantry. Torrejon ordered another attack, this time to the other flank. Cheno, Jose Maria and Tomas could do nothing but watch as, once again, the Americans were able to maneuver their artillery quickly into position and force the Mexican cavalry to retreat in disorder. Cheno felt his jaws muscles clenching. He spit. The American infantry took an offensive formation and advanced to the left of the Mexican army, they were repelled by the artillery. At sunset orders were given to stop hostilities.

"I'm proud of you," General Arista told the commanders. Looking directly to Cheno, he asked. "What's your name, son?"

"Juan Nepomuceno Cortina Goseascochea, General."

Mariano Arista, a strong and slender man in his mid forties, walked up to Cheno; his thick moustache almost covered the grin in his mouth. Extending his hand, he said. "You and your men fought bravely. You showed that you are a good leader. The fatherland will need men of courage and strength, like you. Soon, very soon." Then Arista turned to face the rest of the commanders. "But, now we have to help the wounded and bury the dead. Tonight we'll reorganize our defense in a terrain where they won't be able to mobilize their artillery as well as they did today. We'll be waiting for them at Resaca de la Palma."

"Ignacio, Candelario, Dionaciano, Refugio, Marciano, are all dead." Tomas informed Cheno as they moved to their new position. "Juventino, Arcadio, Miguel and Anastasio are badly wounded. They won't be able to continue. The rest of us are here and ready to fight. How do they move those cannons with such ease? They pounded us badly."

A rattling, melodious sound came from above. "Do you hear that?" Tomas asked.

"It's the breeze through the palm trees, that's all," said Cheno.

"No, it's much more than that. It's an ominous sound. Something bad is about to happen."

"What else could be worse? Be careful now," Cheno said as he led his horse into the water to cross the shallow resaca. Several ducks and a couple of herons flew away. "This is a good spot. We'll rest here tonight. Tomorrow they will come this way; but here they won't be able to maneuver those cannons so easily. Hey, cheer up, old man." Cheno smiled. "Boys, rest now, tomorrow we'll fight again."

The brilliant tone of the morning trumpet called to them. The sun was barely up. Purple and reddish colors surrounded them. The artillery and infantry lined the banks of this former river channel. The heavy Ebony, Mesquite trees and the tall brush covered them. Cheno and the rest of the cavalry took up position in the rear. Flies and mosquitoes took their toll on horses and men, while hundreds of butterflies flew around all of them.

The American attack began with an infantry charge. At the edge, the muddy terrain and the dense brush seemed to contain the strength of the attack, but soon the enemy found a dry crossing. In a flash both sides were engaged in furious hand to hand combat. The dry pathway across the resaca allowed the invaders to easily reach and surround the surprised Mexicans troops. The difficulty of the terrain became more of a burden for the defenders than the attackers. The invader's artillery once again pounded heavily at the Mexican side.

A daring cavalry attack by the Americans captured and silenced the Mexican cannons. The strength of the attack pushed the defending lines back.

"It's time for us to intervene," Cheno told his men.

Almost at the same time, General Arista leading the Tampico battalion came. "They have opened a hole in our lines!" he screamed. "We must go and plug it. Now is when your courage is needed."

Cheno and all of the men spurred their mounts and charged. In an instant Cheno found himself surrounded by furious and fearless enemy soldiers who kept coming. Cheno, Jose Maria and Tomas teamed to contain the attack. They made a good team and made the enemy feel the strength of their arms, it was then that Cheno noticed that General Arista had been surrounded, and although he was fighting hard, he was about to be taken. Cheno screamed to Tomas and Chema. He signaled them toward Arista's location. Understanding, they fought their way toward the General. Simultaneously, the Tampico Battalion was moving in the same direction. All reached the spot and surrounding Arista protected him.

"Save him. Don't let them take him as a prisoner. We'll cover you," Renato Valenzuela yelled to Cheno.

Arista, his eyes wide opened, jaws tight, with his uniform dampened seemed decided to die fighting there. Cheno and Jose Maria swung him on to Tomas' horse who immediately took off to Matamoros.

"The battle is lost. Let's get out of here!" Cheno shouted to Jose Maria and the rest of his men. As they galloped away Cheno is glancing back, saw how the Tampico Battalion although surrounded, kept on fighting. They won't surrender, Cheno thought, feeling sad. As they ran toward the safety of Matamoros, Cheno thought to himself, there must be lots of reasons not to die here today.

The crickets serenaded, as they do every midsummer night. The sweet-bitter odor of the just opened barbacoa pit wafted through the air. The burning taste of the zotol was refreshed by the clay jars. Cheno, Sabas, Jose Maria and Tomas sweated as they enjoyed barbacoa tacos and hot sauce.

"Arista has left for Monterrey and there is a resistance movement being organized," said Tomas.

"The war is over for us," said Sabas as he poured zotol into his jar. "We'll take care of our ranch and try to get along with them."

Cheno and Jose Maria looked at each other. Feeling upset, Cheno took a big gulp of his zotol. It burned all the way down.

CHAPTER 2

The town of Matamoros, at the south shore of the Rio Bravo. Estefana Cortina, accompanied by her sons Cheno, Sabas and Chema and her daughters Refugio and Carmen along with Rafaela, Cheno's fiancé, stood at the French style balcony of the family house just across the Hidalgo plaza. They watched how the American troops marched to the sound of drums and flute through the muddy, oxcart rutted streets. The fearful townsfolk, cautiously curious, observed the parade from the roofs and windows of their adobe and wood homes, but few were on the street. They all observed in silence. Cheno admired how the regular soldiers wore smart blue uniforms and marched in orderly lines, but noticed that the majority, were oddly clad, in wild animal hides and hats with ringed tails. These men marched in absolute disorder and as they marched, they sang, "Green grow the rushes, oh!"

Watching as they shuffled by, a young boy on a nearby roof cried, "mami, mami, I'm scared of those gringos." Those around him, laughed.

"He is right, we all should be afraid," Cheno said, frowning and puffing from his cigar.

"We'll have to learn to get along with them," Sabas replied. "That's all."

"Yes, we'll do just that," Rafaela intervened holding Cheno's hand.

"We'll try," Cheno said, turning to look at her. He smiled, pressing her hand gently.

A few days later, almost at dusk, Cheno and Rafaela strolled along the bank of the Rio Bravo. The sea breeze caressed their faces and tossed Rafaela's long hair, and at the same time, created musical sounds as it sauntered through the Sabal palm fronds. The orange and purple colors of the sunset combined with the greenery of the grass created a sensation of intimacy. It had been a rainy summer swelling the river to its banks. The water looked enticing, tranquil, clean and fresh. Ducks and pelicans swam peacefully.

"What are you thinking, Cheno?" Rafaela asked, reaching for his hand.

"Since the arrival of the gringos there is tension in town," Cheno answered. "Many of my friends are members of the resistance movement," He answered taking her face gently in his hands and looked into her large, black eyes. "I've been asked to join."

"To do that would be foolish," Rafaela responded, letting his hand go. "Wouldn't it be better if you just try to get along?" Her eyes shone looking back at him. "Cheno, ever since I can remember, for one reason or another, you always take up the defense of others. But, let's face it, we have been defeated. You own your ranch, and they don't bother you." She reached for his hands, holding them to her bosom locking on his eyes. "I am hoping that soon we'll get married and begin a large family. Promise me that you won't get involved in that nonsense."

Cheno kept looking straight into her eyes, his gray/green eyes reflecting the colors of the river, when something along the shore drew his attention. "What are they doing?" he asked her.

At some distance, several young Mexican women entered the river, laughing and playfully started washing their legs, long, strong, olive skin legs. They seemed to be having a good time. American soldiers walking toward the bank stopped, surprised. The girls signaled for them to go into the water. Smiling the men doffed their boots, and swam toward the now giggling girls, a promise in their smile. The soldiers approached the girls enjoying the moment. But, when they got close, bullets, coming from the other shore of the river, greeted them.

"Let's get out of here," Cheno said, upset.

. The following Sunday, at Hidalgo's square. The doves in the Cathedral flew as the bells tolled for mass. It was a bright sunny morning. People of all classes, dressed in their best, answered the call. Dona Estefana Cortina and her family were among the faithful.

"Dona Estefana is a pleasure to see you this morning," Rafaela greeted her. She hugged Refugio and Carmen, extending her hand to Cheno, Sabas and Chema who gallantly kissed it. Rafaela and Cheno paired off as they walked together approaching the entrance to the Cathedral.

"You are the best looking charro in town," Rafaela whispered to Cheno who responded by tenderly passing his arm around her shoulders. The silver buttons of his short jacket shone reflecting the flames of the votive candles as they found their place and pew. Respecting custom, and, like everyone else, Cheno didn't carry a pistol to church. Now seated, they were ready to worship.

Everyone stood respectfully as Father Nicolas walked toward and bowed at the altar. At that moment, the sharp sound of hooves in the atrium disrupted the solemnity of the opening Latin phrases. Everyone turned to see what was happening. Three Americans dressed in rags and coon- skin caps grinned cynically as they forced their nervous horses forwards into the sanctuary. Before anyone could react, they were at the altar screaming: "You catholic bastards." Spitting in the face of Father Nicolas, they turned their horses and yelling obscenities, rode out of the Cathedral. Furious, Cheno reached for his Navy Colt, it wasn't there.

That night at a wooden hut just outside town. Tomas Cabrera joined a meeting with members of the resistance movement.

"Hey, Tomas, after what happened today at the Cathedral, I believe Cheno should be ready to join us. With him on our side almost the entire town will get involved in the resistance movement," Pedro Tijerina said as he lighted his cigar on the kerosene lamp.

"Cheno and his family support us. But until now, they do it only morally. As you know, Sabas prefers to get along with the gringos. He says that he is tired with the endless political turmoil and corruption of the Mexican government," Tomas answered reaching for the clay jar of water. "He, like the rest of the rich people is content with the business the Gringos have brought with them." He filled a jarro with water. "Let's give Cheno some time. I'm sure he'll join us."

"We all know how different Sabas and Cheno are," Pedro replied holding the cigar with his teeth.

Looking around, Tomas noticed the seven men present. Three of them, were dressed in charro custom with boots. The others wore huaraches and plain white cotton pants and shirts. He felt comfortable, he was among friends.

"Now, let's talk about our business," Tijerina said, standing to address the group, as he did, he exhaled smoke out his nostrils. Tomas sensed that Tijerina was concerned.

"As you are all aware, yesterday an official shot and killed a barrilero just because he didn't like the water that he had delivered to him." Pedro frowned and looked at Dionaciano Cantu, one of those dressed in charro custom. "Do you think your people could do something about it?" Pedro asked Dionaciano.

"I know the mayor you are talking about. He is a regular at the brothels," Dionaciano replied, also frowning. "Yes, we can take care of him."

"Good, we'll leave that on your hands. Now, let's take of the most important issue. His face softened as he spoke. "As you are also aware, many of the soldiers that have come are Catholics, and a good number of them feel bad fighting under Protestant officers against Catholics. They are willing to switch sides." Now Pedro looked to Juancho, Rafael and Simon, the three in white cotton pants and shirts. "You will be responsible for hiding and guiding them to our troops" The three looked back at Pedro and just nodded.

"Hey, did you noticed the place where the Gringos are building their new fort?" Pantaleon said smiling. "They have chosen low ground. It will get flooded easily."

Tomas looked at him and also smiled. "That could be arranged," he drank his water in a big gulp and then belched.

10

Suddenly, the door was kicked and somebody entered, the darkness of the low entrance masking the newcomer. Everybody jumped, hands to their weapons. Inocencio Flores walked in, he carried a lifeless body in his arms. He had his teeth clenched and tears in his eyes. "This is Juan, my son," he said, as he put the body on the dirt floor. "He was twelve". Today as usual, he went across the river to look after the goats. He got close to the Gringo camp. As he sat watching the animals feed, he was shot. I don't know how many times; Catarino says that he saw how they used him for target practice. A soldier picked him up, put a rifle in his hand and left him in front of Colonel Davenport's quarters. Apparently, he got upset, found me and returned the body. But no one has been punished for the murder of my son."

Tomas Cabrera frowned, fire in his dark eyes. "We'll revenge him," he said.

A few days later, it was late afternoon, at the marketplace. "That's him, now go and charm him" Dionaciano Cantu said to Maria Candelaria, who nodded and walked slowly toward the American officer swinging her hips rhythmically.

"Adios, Senorita," Major Jack Stevenson said, taking his hat off, a broad smile in his face.

"Adios Senor," Maria Candelaria smiled back. Walking slowly, her firm hips moved in a tempting cadence.

Maneuvering himself to her side, Stevenson said, "It's dangerous to walk these streets alone, Senorita. Especially for someone as pretty as you, may I escort you?" His cheeks blushed.

"Thank you. I appreciate your gentleness. But I can take care of myself," Candelaria answered smiling coquettishly. "Perhaps, in another occasion."

"Maybe, tonight?" the mayor asked still smiling and pacing along with her.

"This is where I live. Thank you for your kindness Senor." She blushed and lowered her eyes. "I live with my brother, but he just left for business in Laredo." Now she smiled coyly. "I don't know if I should tell you all this."

"No need to worry, Senorita," Stevenson said. "I won't let you spend the night unprotected."

Candelaria smiled at him, her purple eyes shone before her long eyelashes covered them.

One week later, at the Cortina's family home, the three brothers sat at the kitchen table, enjoying lunch together.

"Colonel Davenport has asked for our help," Sabas said to Cheno and Chema. "One of the American officers is missing." He looked at them and then sipped his horchata.

"Who is he?" Chema asked, chewing his steak.

"Major Jack Stevenson," Sabas answered. "Do you know him?"

11

"I know the man," Cheno said, frowning. "He chases anything with a skirt. Do we have to help them?"

"Yes, we must. It will be good for us if we show our intention of getting along," answered Sabas as he cut his steak.

"I'm not happy helping them. But, I'll take Chema and Tomas with me and find this gringo wherever he is. Most probably recovering from a hangover," Cheno said.

Shortly, after lunch he rode off along with Chema.

"Three days that we have been looking for that man," Cheno said taking his hat of wiping of the sweat from his forehead. "Are you sure you don't know anything about this?" he asked Tomas.

"Why should I know?" Tomas snapped back, reaching for his canteen. Cheno noticed a grin on Tomas' face.

"Hey, look over there," Chema said. "It seems that something is moving on those ebony trees, where the vultures are circling, close to the resaca."

They galloped toward the ebony trees. As they got closer, they noticed a naked body hanging from one of the trees, swaying in the strong breeze.

"That's Major Stevenson," Cheno said as they approached. "This means trouble."

"Madre de Dios!" Chema said. "He's been castrated."

"Well, he got what he deserved," Tomas said as he dismounted and walked toward the body.

They lowered the body and covered it with a sarape.

"Let's take him to the American quarters, they won't like it," Cheno said spitting.

"It will teach them a lesson," Tomas snapped back.

"Let's put the body at the rear of my horse," Chema said, the smell of rotten flesh induced him to spit as well.

Attracted by the smell of the rotten flesh, the vultures had landed and circled around them. Cheno looked at the shore of the resaca and admired how proudly the peacocks fanned their wing tails.

After Major Stevenson's incident, the mistreatment against Mexicans worsened, especially against the peasants. Most of the officers and soldiers of the regular army were respectful of the local customs and even tried to get along with the people. But, those who called themselves volunteers, not members of the regular army respected nothing. They were arrogant, constantly harassing people, trying to pick a fight. They were particularly mean to Mexicans and tejanos of the vaqueros and peasant class. The Gringos, as the blond invaders were now called by the people, shoot peons for no reason, quite often just for target practice. On the Mexican side, the resistance continued, but most of the population made an effort to get along and live in peace.

In spite of the turmoil, business improved. Matamoros located

12

just a few miles inland from the coast, was the port of entrance for supplies for the American troops in Mexico. Thanks to the war there were no taxes, thus many of local merchants profited from the situation, among them the Englishman William Neale, and the American Charles Stillman, the Mexican Iturria brothers, and others like the Spaniard Jose San Roman... Also two Irishmen Richard King and Mifflin Kenedy who came with Taylor built a fortune with a steamboat service on the Rio Bravo. Members of the Cortina family and other prominent Matamoros families also enjoyed the benefits of the economical boom, Sabas and Adolphus Glaevecke, a German immigrant married to Cheno's cousin, made a profit with the sale of horses to the American army. William Neale also improved his business by transporting goods for the troops from the Brazos Santiago at Point Isabel to Matamoros.

Several months after the invasion, the Cortina brothers got together at the family ranch, north of the Rio Bravo. It was a cold winter night.

"I don't know about you," Cheno said, "but I feel bad seeing the mistreatment that most of my friends are receiving. We have been patient. Sabas, you have talked to Colonel Davenport about the volunteers, but, still he has done nothing about them." He paced and kicked a chair angrily. "I say it's time and we join the resistance in an active manner."

"We must be patient," Sabas said. "After Taylor victories in Monterrey and Saltillo, Santa Ana lost the battle at Cerro Gordo, and it seems that this war will end soon" Sabas sighed. "The Americans want not only this land but much more. At the very least they want to make the Rio Bravo the border. Most of our property is north of the river. Even for us, a lot is at stake. So, it's better if we do nothing and get along with them."

"Our great grandparents colonized this land," Chema intervened. "But they did it working along with the people." Standing, he also paced around. "Yes, Sabas, the land is important, and yes, probably it will be better for us if we just get along." He looked to Cheno and Sabas, his black eyes on fire. "But, we also have a duty to our people. They look to us for leadership. I agree with Cheno, we should join the resistance and fight back. We can't just stand by as they step on us."

"Believe me. I feel like you and Cheno," Sabas replied. "But if we take part in this turmoil, things will become worse than they are now. It will be better for everyone if we get along and work with the Americans. I'm sure that once the war is over everything will be different for all of us, including our peones and the poor people. Things will be different for us all. But, first, we must be sure that we are part of whatever system emerges." He smiled. "Relax brothers. On the bright side, as you know the Gringo Fort got flooded. Now there are plans for a new

13

fort in safer and higher ground, and the chosen site happens to be on our property." He stopped looking at his brothers, he looked serious now." Charles Stillman is planning to build a new town around the fort. Business will grow over there, without the high tariff the Mexican government demands. We should all do well. Stillman is already taking care of the deal with Major Chapman who is in charge with the construction of the new fort, which, by the way, it will be named Fort Brown, in memory of an officer who died during the battles in which you took part."

Someone knocked in the door, soft but repeated, nervous knocks. Cheno opened the door. Juana Morales, wife of Tomas Morales, a good friend and rancher, who lived just south of Matamoros, was at the door. Her face was scratched and swollen and her arms covered with bruises. Her dress ripped and she was crying bitterly, she looked devastated.

"Juana, "Cheno said as he gently took her by the hand and lead her into the house. "What happened?"

Juana sobbed having difficulty talking. She made an effort and said, "Please, let me talk to your mother."

"I'll get her," Chema left to look for his mother.

When Dona Estefana arrived, Juana hugged her crying loudly. "Dios mio, Dios mio," she said.

"Ssh, Ssh, come now, sweetheart, relax, please relax," Estefana rubbed Juana's back gently. "Tell me. What happened? Why are you crying this way? Cheno, please get her a chair."

Juana sat at the palm fiber chair offered to her. "The gringos came to my house," Juana started "Oh God, God. Why have you done this to me? to my children?" She cried loudly and sobbed again throwing herself in Estefana's arms. "Why, God. Why?"

Estefana hugged her gently, caressing her back. She looked at her sons and signaled for them to stay silent and sit. They obeyed.

"They entered suddenly, destroying the door and everything in their way," Juana continued as she finally relaxed a bit. "'Where is he?' they cried slapping me on the face. When Teresa and Maruja came to my defense, they also beat them. Tomas was out milking the goats, came running as soon as he heard the noise. When he walked in, they beat him, kicked him violently, screaming: 'Where are the others? Who are you accomplices?' Juana looked sadly to the floor before continuing.

"I don't know, Senor. I don't understand. Why are you here? What are you talking about?' Tomas tried to answer."

"'Don't lie to us, you son of a bitch,' they said. 'We know that you are one of them. You are one of those who have ambushed us. You are a spy for the Mexicans. You have helped those damn Catholic's deserters to join your army.' They kept telling him."

14

"Tomas said, 'that's not true I just want to live in peace here at my ranch, I really don't know what you are talking about'."

"You are a liar," they said. 'Tell us about Cheno Cortina. We know that you are a good friend of him. The whole town talks about him. Is he a member of the resistance? Is he your leader? Speak up you damn greaser.'They all talked at the same time that they beat him. Oh my dear Tomas," she cried again.

"I don't know." She continued repeating Tomas words. "I don't know anything." As far as I know Cheno is not a member of any resistance. He and his family are trying to cooperate as most of us are." Tomas told them over and over, but they wouldn't listen."

"You are lying, but we'll teach you and all of your kind a lesson." Then, one of them looked at me and the girls. "Oh God, God, Why have you done this to us? Why?"Juana cried loudly.

Cheno got up, walked to her and held her hands. "Calm yourself, you are among friends. Relax now and tell us: What happened?"

"Oh God, God,"Juana continued crying. She took a deep breath: "'Tie him,' one of them said. Then he went and pulled me by the hair. When the girls cried, they slapped them. He, that beast, ripped my clothes and forced himself into me. Afterwards, they took turns on me. Others went to the girls and did the same to them. Tomas screamed all the time, but they just laughed. Finally, one of them shot Tomas and they left. I don't know how, but I managed to run to Catarino's and got help. Fortunately Tomas is alive. Dr. Wallace says that he'll survive. Thank God he is strong. Dr. Wallace asked me to come and tell you about this."

Cheno's stare passed her, the tears running down his cheek made his red beard shine. Suddenly, he stood up, "Chema, get the guns," he yelled.

"Wait," Sabas said. "Juana what has happened to you is a disgrace. We'll not let it go unpunished, I promise. But," turning and talking to Cheno, "guns are not the way. We'll not go anywhere if we take that route. We'll talk to Colonel Davenport. I'm sure he'll make justice for all."

Two days later, at the American headquarters Sabas, Cheno and Chema told Juana's story to Colonel Davenport.

"We are looking for justice, Colonel," Cheno said as he stared straight into Davenport's eyes.

"Yes, Senor Cortina, rest assured, whoever did this will be severely punished," Davenport replied. "General Taylor left specific instructions to keep peace and respect your properties and customs, and I plan to follow his orders." Cheno perceived the odor of booze as Davenport spoke. "Cheap whiskey," Cheno thought.

"I'm glad to hear that, Colonel, I was certain that you would not allow as serious a crime as this, to go unpunished." Sabas was quick to intervene. "My brothers and I appreciate your help. We are certain that we can learn to live together and in peace."

"Yes, I'm also certain that we'll learn," Davenport answered, smiling.

"Well, we won't take any more of your time," Sabas said extending his hand.

"This problem will be taken care of immediately," Davenport said as he shook hands with Sabas.

When they were at the door, Cheno overheard Colonel Davenport calling Chapman. "Major," he said, "Find out which men were involved in the Morales ranch deal and send them immediately to join Taylor wherever he might be."

CHAPTER 3

"Hey, Pantaleon, the horses will be here soon. Be sure the fence is firm," Cheno whispered as he maneuvered to hide on top of a mesquite tree branch.

It had been another rainy summer. The entire valley was full of small lagoons. The grass was high, and the wild horses were roaming freely. Cheno, Pantaleon, Refugio and Dionaciano were waiting for them. Cheno climbed to the top of a mesquite tree with a lariat at his side. Pantaleon was hiding behind the false fence he had built around the small lagoon, leaving only one side open for the horses to approach. Refugio and Dionaciano hide at the entrance of the trap, to prevent the escape of the horses. It was late in the evening.

The leader of the herd, a palomino, cautiously approached the lagoon, always vigilant, stepped into the water, while the others waited. The mustang was strong, of small frame, but agile and athletic. Cheno held his breath, readying his rope. He observed as the mustang signaled to the herd and the wild horses moved toward the water.

A young line back dun horse stood out. Like the leader, he was a strong horse but more nervous and agile. As he drank, he frequently moved his head up, eyes staring, ears twitching back, muscles tense. Suddenly a lariat got around his neck. He tried to run, but Cheno jumped down from the tree and passed the rope around the horse's front leg, forcing him to stumble. In the blink of an eye the horse was tied to the tree, held by his neck and a front leg.

Pantaleon, Refugio and Dionaciano meanwhile surrounded two other horses, letting the rest go. Being seasoned vaqueros soon they had horses securely tied to a tree.

"Great," Cheno said, "now, let them rest for today. Tomorrow, we'll break them."

"We deserve a good sotol," said Refugio as he sat on the grass and pulled a clay jar to his lips and downed a big gulp.

The following day, they rose before sunrise to a steaming cup of coffee and a breakfast of beef jerky, hot sauce and flour tortillas, getting ready for the task ahead.

"Remember, Cheno, first, let the horse know you." Dionaciano, the eldest of the group, smiled revealing gaps where his teeth used to be.

"How many times have you told me the same thing, Chano?" Cheno answered, before sipping his coffee, holding the tin cup with both hands.

"Yes, I'm getting old," Dioanciano (Chano to his friends) replied. "Since you were a little child you have preferred to be with us, the vaqueros, instead of playing with your brothers and the other children." The creases in his skin looked like deep grooves in his tanned face. He sipped his coffee.

Refugio and I will take care of the palomino and the bay horses," Pantaleon intervened, "so you, Cheno, can work on the dun and Chano will help wherever he is needed." He took a bite of his dry meat. His black moustache moving rhythmically as he chewed. "So, what do you think?"

"Fine, let's start," Cheno said. Finishing his coffee, he stood and walked toward the horses so as not to frighten them. The others followed him.

Cheno approached the dun horse, letting the animal size him up. The horse stood expectant, head up, ears forward, muscles tense.

"Hello, friend," Cheno said standing in front of the dun being sure that the horse had a good look of him. "We are going to work together. You will understand that we are friends, and we are going to stay that way forever. From now on, your name is Palomo, Palomo, do you understand?"

Cheno caressed the horse slowly, gently, using his bare hand first, moving slowly, slowly, ever so slowly, around the horse, whispering to him constantly, making sure that the horse remained relaxed. Then, always gently, he let the animal feel the rope. After a while, the horse had accepted a bridle into which Cheno had added a cover for the eyes. Pulling the eye cover down, carefully tenderly, he put the saddle atop the horse. He climbed the mesquite tree, whistling to Chano to let the horse's leg go free. Then, he pulled up the eye cover and mounted.

As soon as he felt the weight on his back, the dun curved it and jumped with all four legs attempting to get rid of the undesired weight. Cheno was ready and held firm. Two, three, four times, the horse bounced fiercely. Cheno held on. Finally the dun made a furious jump and Cheno flew off his back. Chano with a firm hold in the rope was ready for and immediately passed the rope around the horse's legs and tied it to the tree.

"It's a great horse, we'll get along," Cheno said, a satisfied grin on his face. "Hold it, let's try it again." He repeated the routine, when he felt the horse was comfortable, he mounted him as Chano freed the horse's leg. As soon as the dun felt the extra weight on his back, he arched it and jumped high in the air. This time, Cheno held on for eight jumps before he ended head over knees in the lagoon. The whitetail ducks startled and flew away circling the pond once before gliding to a safer place, away from the vaqueros.

"Woohoow," Cheno screamed. "This is great. Let's do it again."

18

Three days later, the horses had not only accepted a raider on their backs, but they obeyed orders guiding the cows just as if that was what they had been doing their entire lives. The dun was the last one to surrender to his trainer, and even then, he would accept only Cheno as his master.

At sunset of the third day, they rested as a goat was being roasted for dinner. "Listen, somebody is coming. Probably Indians," Refugio said.

"I can hear the horses," Pantaleon said, "but how do you know they are Indians?"

"They don't shoe their horses," Refugio answered.

A group of five Comanche approached. Proceeding slowly and deliberately, they rode straight, proud, both hands on the horses.

"Saludos," their leader said in Spanish.

"Saludos," Cheno answered, extending his right arm inviting them to share the dinner.

The Comanche dismounted and joined the party. Their bodies were slender, strong, but with the collar bones too prominent. "You are a great horse tamer," the leader said to Cheno, after he sat, crossing his legs, keeping his body straight and alert. "We have been watching you for the last two days." He looked to the horses, his expression betraying sadness." We need horses, but we have almost nothing to offer you in trade."

"Your Spanish is good," Dionaciano said. "Why do you need the horses?"

"The Padres taught us at the mission. We were at peace there. When you came, we fought, but thanks to the Padres we learned to live if not together, at least we didn't bother each other." His face turned hard. "But now, the White men have come and they share nothing" The other Comanche raised their chins as they heard their leader. Their faces also hard. "When a small group of renegades attacked a train going to El Paso, the White men retaliated attacking our village, killing everything that moved." He looked out to the distance. "We are traveling with our families to the mission in Parras. Hopefully we'll have peace again there."

Pantaleon and Refugio had finished roasting the goat, sliced it, and started passing the pieces among the Comanche. Dionaciano offered some sotol to wash it down.

"I'm sorry and understand your sorrows," Cheno looked straight in the eyes of the Comanche leader. "You can have two of the horses we just tamed." He looked towards the other horses. "You may pick one of those horses, too. Don't worry about trade now." He shrugged his shoulders. "Who knows? Perhaps in the future we'll be in need and you could help us then."

The Comanche looked back at Cheno, "You are a good man."

He pulled a small stone talisman from around his neck and offered it to Cheno. "If you are ever in need of help, just show this to any Comanche."

"Thanks," said Cheno accepting the offer. "I'm glad to help you." He put the lace with the totem around his neck carefully, with respect.

"Someone is coming fast, probably a Mexican," Refugio said

"Yeah, his horse has shoes, eh?" Pantaleon said, a sarcastic grin in his face.

"You'll see," Refugio answered.

Tomas Cabrera, riding at full gallop arrived. "Cheno, Sabas has sent me looking for you." He said as soon as he had dismounted. "The war is over. You are needed for an urgent family reunion."

Cheno smiled and offered Tomas a leg of the roasted goat. "You look tired. Come and join us, we'll leave tomorrow."

At Guadalupe Hidalgo, Mexico, a treaty was signed. Mexico recognized defeat and accepted the Rio Bravo as the boundary between the two countries. The United States not only got the Rio Grande Valley as part of its territory, but also Arizona, New Mexico, Colorado, California and part of what is now Utah, Nevada and Wyoming. Mexico accepted 20,000 dollars as payment for this land. However, at the same time, they agreed to pay US expenses for the war for the same sum.

Mexican citizens with properties north of the Rio Grande would be allowed to retain their properties as long as they were able to prove ownership to the satisfaction of the American authorities. If they chose to stay they would become American citizens automatically after two years.

"Cheno, I'm happy to see you here son," Dona Estefana said smiling as she walked towards him; she hugged and kissed him in the cheek, her gray eyes shining. "Your opinion will help us to reach, what I hope will be the right decision."

Present at the reunion were Sabas, Cheno, Chema and their sisters Refugio and Carmen. Also Rafaela and her parents were there. The men smoked fine cubanos.

"I invited these gentlemen," Estefana continued, pointing to Charles Stillman, Francisco Iturria and Adolphus Glaevecke. The first was an American businessman established in Matamoros. The second a Mexican, who was also a prominent young businessman and had learned the trade from Stillman, and the last was a member of the Cortina family through marriage. "I believe their opinion will also be helpful."

"Mama," Sabas opened the discussion, "I would like to remind everybody that the Espiritu Santo grant is mostly north of the river." He stood up, letting his already prominent belly show. "There are more than 150,000 acres of good land there," he continued. "Although we

20

also own some good property in the south side, it doesn't make sense to give up what has been in the family for several generations." He took a puff of his cigar, looking up. "In a way this war has been a blessing for the family. Now, we'll have political stability. If we get along with the new authorities, our chances for economic growth are better than ever." He walked toward a table and left his cigar on an ash tray, then he sat again.

"He is right," Stillman said, "it would be foolish on your part to abandon what is yours." He sipped his coffee. "My lawyers have reviewed with Dona Estefana the papers. It shouldn't be any problem to prove ownership." He paused and then, addressing all the present, continued. "With the construction of Fort Brown a golden opportunity has opened for all." He took a deep breath, looked down for a moment and then lifting his head, he continued. "I believe that it is possible to create a new town, taking advantage of the protection of the fort and its continuous need for supplies." He paused for a moment, looking around to all of those present. "Part of the site that I propose for this town is also on your property, Dona Estefana. My lawyers have already helped you with the deal for the construction of the fort, and they will be glad to help you once again."

"We're in," Glaevecke said in his harsh Spanish, with a strong German accent. "Concha's grant is also on the north side of the river." His already red cheeks blushed. "Many of the Mexicans will choose the south side of the river or simply go south, so there is going to be a lot of property available at cheap prices," He smiled showing his teeth stained with tobacco and sipping his zotol he continued. "Also, there are more cattle roaming free than ever, just waiting for someone to put his brand on them."

"What about the people?" Chema asked. "Yes, this is a good time for those who are in advantageous position. But, what about the peons, the barrileros, the vaqueros?" He stared at them, especially at Cheno and Sabas. "What about the people who have worked with us for all of these years?" Standing he paced around the room. "Before, we had some minor difficulties," he continued, "but since the arrival of the troops, a lot of civilians have followed, many of them outlaws, and the numbers of brothels and cantinas have increased." Now he focused on Stillman and Iturria, "I understand that your business has improved as well as ours." Then he pointed toward his mother, cautiously. "I also understand that the creation of a new town will bring a lot of more business opportunities for our family, yes since the proposed town is on our property it will be good for us." Putting his hand down, he hesitated for a moment. "But we are Mexicans, and we have been badly mistreated in our own land. As we all know the authorities have done nothing to protect the rights of our people. They pretend to listen to us when we have complained, but nothing has changed."

"That's all true, brother," Cheno said. "And that is precisely why we must stay on the north side of the river." Puffing his cigar he was bold in his pronouncement. "Precisely for those reasons we must ensure that our people are treated justly." He sipped his zotol. "We'll learn their laws, we'll take part in politics, and we'll be sure that indeed all are treated as Americans."

Rafaela smiled clapping her hands with admiration.

"Well said," Stillman also clapped his hands, "Indeed, that's the sprit. You can count on me to help. What do you think, Francisco?" He looked at Iturria.

"Certainly, I agree with everything. This is a great opportunity for all of us, and in particular I like the idea of a new town. And of course I also agree with what Cheno said."

"Well, it seems that everybody is in agreement," Estefana said. "We'll move to the north side of the river, but also keep our property in the south side." She then looked to Chema and Cheno. "You two will take care of that part of the property."

"We'll do it," Chema said. "Our primos from the Trevino and Gomez families will help."

"Yes, we'll be Americans." Cheno sighed. Rafaela took his hand tenderly.

"A toast," Sabas said standing up and extending his right arm holding a glass of wine.

Everyone also stood up, extending their arms, glasses full. .

"To Mexico, our old country," Sabas said. "And to the United States of America, our new country." He drank. Everyone else joined.

CHAPTER 4

"Look George, this is going to be a modern town it will have wide streets and alleys to access the buildings from the rear." Charles Stillman said, pointing at the plan that was extended at his desk. "There is no need for the streets to radiate from a central square, like here in Matamoros. And let's not worry about public buildings now, but do reserve four blocks for a square." It's going to be a beautiful town. My town, he thought

"I have planned other cities before." George Lyons, deputy surveyor for the Nueces County, assured him. "Of course, there is also a need for a market. Let's put it here," he added marking a cross on the design.

Charles Stillman handled a trade family business that extended from almost all of Mexico and the eastern United States, with offices in New York and New Orleans. He handled the Mexican side of it from his two story brick building, across from plaza Hidalgo in Matamoros. His own office was in the second floor. From there, he could observe not only the movement in town, but also the boats on the river. Now he was planning a new town, on the northern bank of the river. The war was a stroke of luck for me, he thought, I will now handle the business from the American side, with the protection of the American Army and without paying the high tariff imposed by the Mexicans. He smiled.

"Shouldn't we assure our title to the property first?" Samuel Belden asked as he poured a cup of coffee.

"I have already paid some Mexicans for their part of the ejido; I even bought land from David Snearly, an American." Stillman replied, "Basse and Hord are already handling the legal claim of property with the owners of the Espiritu Santo grant, so all sides are covered. I'm so sure that I already have names for the streets." He smiled proudly. "The three main streets will be named Elizabeth, St. Francis and St. Charles, and of course there will be a Levee street to give access to the river boats. The rest will be named after the American Presidents. This is going to be the business of our lifetime."

"St. Francis after your father, St. Charles after yourself," Belden said. "Elizabeth, is it after your bride to be?"

Stillman just grinned. Maybe it should be named Isabel, he thought, after my beautiful Mexican.

"Mr. Stillman, there is a Mr. Mussina asking to talk to you," an assistant said, entering the office. "He says that he wants to talk to you about the new town around Fort Brown, and that he has bought part of the proposed site from Manuel Trevino Canales and Andres Fragoza."

"What?" Stillman said almost jumping around the heavy oak desk. "How does he know about it?" He turned to Belden. "How did you miss that? I asked you to take care of that part of the deal."

"The Mussina brothers are traders from New Orleans who have been buying land at Point Isabel," Belden replied. "I thought I had a deal with Canales and Fragoza, but the brothers must have offered more money. Let's see what he has to offer."

"Show him in," Stillman ordered the clerk.

Simon Mussina accepted a chair, a cup of coffee and a cigar before beginning. "As you do, Mr. Stillman," he said, "my brother and I believe that there is an opportunity for business and development here." He smoked his cigar and passed his left hand over his thick, black moustache. "This is the natural route for business from New Orleans into Mexico, so we have been buying land in Point Isabel. When we heard about the construction of Fort Brown and the plan for a town around it, we thought that it would be good idea for us to get involved." He smiled. "We already know that you have secured most of the property and that you have Major Chapman in your pocket, but now we are in possession of an important portion of the property involved. But, there is no need to worry." He paused for a moment, looking at Stillman. "We are businessmen and that's the reason I'm here now. Hopefully we'll get along and reach a satisfactory deal."

Stillman rocked in his chair, staring back at Simon Mussina, while puffing on his cigar. He realized that Mussina had the upper hand for the time being. I need time, he thought. Then he stood up, extended his right hand to Mussina. "We'll make a deal," he said.

Mussina smiled and took Stillman's hand.

"Would it be fine with you if we include Mr. Belden?" Stillman said, pointing toward Samuel Belden, who smiled and waived his hand. "Also, we'll have to include Major Chapman in the deal, off the record, of course. So, if it's agreeable each will have 25% of the company, although, in paper, I'll have 50%. Agreed?"

"Agreed," Mussina said smiling. "Of course we'll have a legal contract."

"That's out of question. The office of Basse and Hord will take care of the legal aspect. Let's have a drink to it." Stillman put three cognac glasses on the desk and poured a little into each.

"To the Brownsville Town Company," Belden said lifting his glass.

"The lots are selling well. Iturria and San Roman among many others Matamoros businessmen have paid in cash the fifteen hundred dollars we are asking. Even Kenedy and King the steam boat owners have bought lots. They also have a bar. Well, really, a brothel in disguise.

24

Those are astute businessmen; it would be good for you to partner with them. You should be happy to know that already there is a lot of construction going on. The fact that you are already building your house and an office over there has helped." Robert Hord, Stillman's assistant in charge of developing the town, said to Stillman. "But there is an important legal problem that you must be made aware of," he added as he wiped the sweat from his forehead. "Rafael Garcia Cavazos has changed his mind and now does not agree to sell his part of the property. He has hired W.G. Hale and has started a legal suit, claiming that the ejido titles you and Mussina bought are illegal because the sellers did not own the land, but were only sharecroppers for their legitimate owners. And to top that Dona Estefana is hesitant to sign her part of the deal. She says that her children will not agree to the sum of one dollar as payment for the portion of land that is included."

Stillman, hand on his chin, rocked in his chair. His blue eyes looked off into the distance, then, he slowly turned hid head to look straight at Hord. "Do you have seventeen thousand dollars?" he said without blinking.

"No, I don't. Why do you ask?" Hord replied.

Stillman grinned. "It really doesn't matter; in fact this only simplifies the situation and gives us the opportunity to get rid of the Mussina brothers." He stood up and walked toward the window. His brisk walking caused a loud sound when his boots hit the wooden floor. Looking out to the Hidalgo plaza, the cathedral, and in the distance, the American flag flying over Fort Brown, he pointed toward the town under construction, the grin from his face gone. "You and Elisha will buy the Company from us. Since the papers of Canales and Fragoza are worthless, the Mussina brothers can be left out of the deal." Turning around his blue eyes pierced Hord's. "Do you follow, Robert?" Hord nodded. "Offer Cavazos twenty- five thousand dollars for his part of the property; you could raise it up to thirty- five, if necessary. Then explain to Dona Estefana that she could lose the entire hundred-fifty thousand acres if she doesn't agree to give a little to the community. She is smart, and will understand."

"Aren't you worried about her children's reaction to the sale?" Hord asked.

"I can deal with Sabas and his sisters. They are civilized people. Even Jose Maria can be talked to. Cheno is the wild one, he could give us trouble. But, I'll handle him when the time comes. Now that we mention him, I haven't seen him for a while."

"Cheno I'd like to thank you for coming along," Captain John J. Dix said. "We need someone who knows not only how to handle horses, but also how to deal with the vaqueros."

"I'm glad to help you and the Army" Cheno replied. They were leading the seventy five wagon train carrying Army supplies from

25

Matamoros to San Antonio, plus a herd of over one thousand horses and the necessary mules for changing teams as necessary. "Although it seems to me that not everybody is happy with your decision to make me second in command, especially captain Ives."

"You'd better get used to it. You were a Mexican fighting us, and now you have chosen to become an American by joining our Army. There are those who won't understand it. Especially among the Americans who fought in the war. But, even they will have to understand that the Army chooses the best man for a job. And you are the best for this one. Although, I'm aware that some people coming from up north will resent it, I have given strict orders that you personally must authorize and supervise every change of teams. That way I'll be sure that the animals aren't abused."

"I appreciate your confidence in me. We'll be in Goliad soon," Cheno said, "I'll check the teams there."

The muddy, heavily thicketed trail made handling of the heavy wagons difficult. Cheno noticed that some of the wagon masters abused their mules, whipping them harder than they should.

"Hey, be careful!" Cheno shouted to one of the wagon masters, a recent Texan, originally from New York. "There is no need to beat them. They obey if you are gentle with them."

"No greaser is going to tell me how to handle a mule," the wagon master answered in a harsh tone of voice, whipping the animals even harder. "I treat mules the same way I treat Mexicans." He stared at Cheno, as if challenging him.

Cheno went to his gun, but, noticed something was slowing down the train. He glared back at the wagon master, and pulling the reins of his dun, galloped toward the front of the train. Approaching he noticed that a small band of Lipan Apaches, native to the area, who always traveled on foot, were approaching the train. They were mostly women and children. They were in rags and appeared both, tired and hungry. Some of the men from the train were screaming at them and one of them reached for his gun.

"Hold it!" Cheno shouted to the men, galloping to the head of the train and toward the Apache group.

The Lipan could do nothing but stand aside wide eyed and trembling.

"Where are you headed?" Cheno asked the eldest woman in Spanish.

"To the mission in Parras," she answered. "We are hungry. Could you give us some food?"

Cheno nodded. "Rest here with us." He turned in his saddle toward one of the vaqueros, "Juancho, give these people some food."

"Why should we stop for these filthy Indians?" one of the wagon masters asked, spitting on the ground.

26

"You don't give orders here, you take them," Cheno replied. "We are going to share our food with them. Do you have any objections?"

"What's going on?" Dix asked as he approached the Anglo wagon master.

"We ain't taking orders from this greaser," one of the wagon masters said.

"He wants us to stop for these filthy Indians," one of the teamsters added. "And, to top that, he wants us to give them food."

"What happened, Cheno?" Dix asked.

Cheno explained to Dix the reasons for his orders.

"Cortina is the second in command here," Dix said after listening to Cheno. "It's time for us to rest a little. These people are peaceful. They are hungry. Give them something to eat as Cheno said."

"Let the Mexicans do it," Captain Ives said. "They enjoy eating the same shit."

After a short while, they continued their way. The train traveled slowly. The humid heat made it even more difficult. The mules pulled hard. The men damped by sweat, yelled and swore to make them to pull even harder. The buzzing mosquitoes tortured everyone.

"Come on," Ives screamed, "make those mules move, hit them hard, so they will pull."

"There is no need to hurry. Be gentle with the animals and they will move steadily." Cheno repeated. Some of the wagon masters obeyed Ives but the majority listened to Cheno seeing reason in his orders. The air was hot and humid, even Cheno who was used to the fierce climate felt his skin burning. Although he was sweating profusely, his mouth was dry and burned every time he swallowed the salty saliva.

The sun was setting when they arrived at Goliad. Some of the wagon masters and teamsters, who had forced their mules, were asking for a change of teams.

"Before you get a new team, it has to be approved by Cortina," the Mexican herder in charge of the mules said.

"What?" One of the wagon masters, a tall, corpulent man, complained. "No greaser is going to tell me when it's time to change my team. Give me those mules or I'll kill you on the spot."

"You will kill no one, and you are not getting any mules either," Cheno said walking toward the man.

"You damn son of a bitch, I have had enough of you." The big man threw a right hand punch. Cheno easily moved to the side. The man's enormous fist missed him. Cheno swung around, kicking him between the legs. The giant fell to the ground groaning and turning blue. Cheno stepped behind him and clamped an arm around his throat.

"Let go Cheno, you are going to kill him," Dix said as he rushed over to pull Cheno away.

"I won't tolerate anyone talking to me like that." Cheno said. "Besides you gave me orders to take care of the teams, and I'm going to do that. These men have got to learn to respect me."

"These Mexicans are trouble makers," Ives said as he approached the group.

"No, they are not," Dix answered, "and now they are also Americans, working for the American Army. We must learn to respect each other and work together.

"That ain't never going to happen," the wagon master grunted, as he struggled to his feet, still blue and holding his hand between his legs. "These greasers won't ever be the same as us." Cheno and the other Mexicans stared at him, and some started to go for their guns. Cheno and Dix signaled them to hold on. They all walked away peacefully.

The following morning Cheno went through each team and allowed those that needed to be changed. Reluctantly, and at the request of Dix, Cheno agreed to change the team of the corpulent wagon master who had caused trouble the day before. Although everybody worked as usual, Cheno noticed that Mexicans and Americans were viewing each other cautiously, with resentment and distrust.

It was late in the afternoon when Dix approached Cheno. "I am going to go on to visit my parents at La Grange; I'll meet you there tonight. In my absence Captain Ives will be in charge. I trust that you will get along with him," Dix said before leaving.

"Go in peace. We'll get along fine. And say hello to your parents for me," Cheno answered.

"Thank you I'll do that."

As they approached La Grange the same wagon master who had already changed teams came to ask for a new team.

"I'm sorry, but I have already told you that I can't give you new mules without the approval of Senor Cortina," the herder told the man.

"And I have already told you that no mule is going to tell me when it's time to change teams," the wagon master replied slapping the herder, who fell to the ground, his nose and mouth bleeding. When, he tried to get up, the big wagon master kicked him back to the ground.

The noise made others gather around. "And as for you, son of a bitch," the wagon master screamed as soon as he saw Cheno coming at a run. "Come here, I'll show you how I treat the damn mules."

"Leave now and in peace," Cheno said as he approached. "I don't want any more trouble."

"You are a coward, I don't bother with cowards," the wagon master growled. "We defeated you in war. We are your masters and I'll teach you to show respect."

"I respect those who respect others," Cheno said walking slowly toward him. The sharp, musical sound of his Spanish steel spurs added drama to the moment.

The big bully kicked at Cheno, who slid under the man's boot

28

and hit the big man directly in the nose, cracking it. A torrent of blood flowed.

"Hold it!" screamed Captain Ives as Cheno was about to strike again. "What's going here?"

"These greasers are again refusing to change the mules as we need them," the wagon master answered. "They believe that because we have allowed them to work for us, they are like us," he added, spitting blood.

"You are a trouble maker," Ives said pointing to Cheno. "Give him the mules he is requesting."

"Captain Dix put me in charge of the mules and horses," Cheno answered, "this man just changed teams in Goliad, the mules in his team are fresh."

"I am in charge now," Ives replied, "and I order you to release the mules."

"If we are not going to get the respect we deserve, we'll leave as soon as Captain Dix comes back," Cheno said.

The following morning, Captain Dix was informed of the situation. He decided that it would be better to discharge Cheno and his men from the Army.

"I'm sorry to let you go, you are a good man and a good leader. But, unfortunately, the moment is not appropriate. You and your men will be discharged honorably and paid. Give this letter to the pay master in Brownsville once you get there. What are your plans now?" Dix asked Cheno, handling him the letter to the paymaster.

"I'll go back home and start my own ranching business, continue helping my mother and hopefully, get married as soon as possible," Cheno answered, taking the letter and smiling at Dix. They hugged each other, and Cheno mounted Palomo and ordered his men back to Brownsville.

"Once we are back in Brownsville," Cheno told his men as they galloped back, "I'll start my own ranching. I will be honored if you accept working for me as vaqueros."

"You should already know that we are loyal to you. Of course you can always count on us." One of the men answered, for all of therm.

Cheno smiled. "And of course you are all invited at the time of my wedding."

"Cheno, I'm happy to see that you are going to start your own ranching business and your own family. You know how we all feel about Rafaela and her family" Dona Estefana said. "You could take the San Jose area that you like so much, and that way you will be between Sabas and the part where we are now." She hesitated for a moment. "But, there is something that you must know."

"What is it?" Cheno asked feeling worried at her tone.

"Mr. Hord has informed us that there are some problems with the legal recognition of the family grant. Sabas, Chema and your sisters have agreed to the deal that Senor Stillman has proposed through him. I hope that you will also agree."

Cheno frowned, his right hand moving out of habit toward his beard. "What is the deal," he asked.

Estefana told him the details of the proposal. Cheno listened respectfully to his mother as his jaws tightened. He pulled at his beard. He didn't blink while Dona Estefana talked nor did he interrupt her.

"So, what do you think?" she asked when she finished.

"Do we have a choice?" Cheno asked back, his gray-green eyes piercing through her. "They have the upper hand, at least for now."

CHAPTER 5

Cheno and Rafaela rode their horses at a leisurely pace. The sun was shining and the sea breeze made it a pleasant morning. The orange, blue and gray clouds in the blue sky formed capricious figures. Cheno was riding Palomo, his favorite dun and rode straight in his Mexican saddle, a broad hat on his head. Rafaela rode a palomino in side saddle style. A skillful rider she looked elegant in her bright- colored dress. Her long, black hair shone, sparkling shades of blue and purple, a beautiful Amazon.

"Look how high the grass is," Cheno said. "It's perfect for cattle and horses. Besides, it will let us have a large goat and wool sheep herd, there is plenty of grass for all." He breathed in, since he was a child, he had learned to love this land, and the thought that it soon would be the place where they would be raising a family made him happy. He held his horse in front of a humble wooden- stick hut with a roof made of palm tree leaves. "This is the place," Cheno said, dismounting, "I know that it is just a shack now, but by the time we are married it will be a nice wood and adobe house with clean and firm brick and wooden floors."

"I love it," Rafaela said. "It's in a beautiful spot." She looked at the green grass and the gentle slope toward a resaca that was full with rain water, lilies floating on the surface and a couple of herons stood at the shore, the air smelled clean. "This is a perfect place for raising children." She added.

They walked to the hut. "Cheno, I 'm so happy, that I could scream. I love you so much," she said as she hugged and kissed him. Cheno hugged and kissed her deeply, feeling happy with the strength of the moment. Rafaela pulled away. "Enough of that," she said, "You'll have to wait until we get married."

Cheno laughed. "Of course, you know that I love and respect you, we'll wait." Then he looked around. "Now I have to think about getting enough cattle to graze this land. Cousin Adolphus has offered me the sale of some good cows that he got from Mexico."

"I don't trust him. He is always so mellow with the wealthy, but harsh and mean with the peons. He is not like you. Be careful of him."

"He has good contacts on both sides of the river. Besides don't forget. He is married to my cousin."

"But," she warned. "People say that he buys stolen cattle from Mexico."

31

"I'll be careful," Cheno said, holding her hand. "I'll look at that cattle and if they're good and he can prove to me they're not stolen, I might buy them." Cheno, although still was holding her hand, his mind suddenly went somewhere else. "What really worries me is the way Brownsville and Matamoros are growing. There are a lot of new comers, most of them troublesome." He let her hands go and walked out of the hut. "Thanks to them we have many more bars and brothels and I don't like the methods Marshall Shears is using to keep a semblance of peace. In particular I am concerned about the way he uses those wild dogs. Several good vaqueros have been seriously injured by them, most of them for no fault of their own."

"Just be patient most of them are just passing through, on their way to California," Rafaela replied. "Almost nobody likes Shears methods, but he has the support of Senor Stillman and others like Richard King and Miflin Kenedy

" Funny that you mention them," Cheno said, " because I'm concerned about the way that Stillman and his new partners, King and Kenedy are getting land and cattle from Mexicans who have been forced to go south by legal or scare tactics and Shears is good at the last."

Rafaela stared at him, horrified. "Juan Nepomuceno Cortina," she screamed. "Don't start getting involved where you're not invited." Cheno frowned; feeling troubled, then, her voice softened. "We are talking about getting married and raising children. Please, just worry about that."

"You know how much I love you" Cheno replied. "But also, I care for the people. You already know that I'm planning to get involved in politics. Yes, I want to prosper and live in peace, but I'll do my best to be sure that all are treated fairly."

Rafaela sighed. "You'll never change." She kissed him tenderly on his chin.

One hundred mooing long horns roamed in a fenced field near Brownsville. "These cattle are healthy, no ticks on them. I can guarantee it," Adolphus Glaevecke said smiling at Cheno, Chema and Tomas.

"Sure, they look healthy, but they have a Mexican brand," Chema said as he scraped the dung from his boot on the fence rail. "How did you get them?"

"My partners in Mexico Jean Vela and Tomas Vazquez took care of the deal for me," Glaevecke answered, "I have full confidence in them, it's all legal."

"I wouldn't be sure," Chema said to Cheno, "something doesn't seem right, Vela and Vazquez are those who are in charge of branding cattle for King and Kenedy and everybody knows that they brand any animal that crosses their way. These are great cattle. But, why would Garza sell them? Why didn't they offer them to their bosses?"

32

"As you know," Glaevecke intervened, "the Garza family got in financial trouble when they chose to go south. The cattle came to us simply because we offered a better deal."

Tomas stared at Glaevecke. "It's really strange that King just got the Mendiola's land for peanuts and now the Garza's are selling their cattle in Mexico" Cabrera jumped the fence, strode over to the cattle and examined several of the cows. "Indeed these cattle are healthy and in great shape," he said.

Cheno also jumped the fence and went to the cattle examining several of the animals himself. "They look good. Do you have the proper receipt of the sale from Garza?"

"Of course," Glaevecke answered a broad smile on his face. "Vazquez paid the one hundred Pesos in gold for the lot; here is the receipt."

"We have a deal then," Cheno said, "I'll buy from you fifty of these cows as long as you let Tomas choose them. Is that all right with you?"

"Sure," Glaevecke answered extending his right hand.

Cheno and Glaevecke shook hands vigorously, wide smiles on their faces.

"Are you sure Cheno?" Tomas asked, a little later.

"Yes, these are good cattle, and he has the receipt. Besides, in spite of the rumors, Adolfo has gained the trust of Mama, so I will also trust him. Pay him," Cheno said "Then let's go to Catchel's place and enjoy a good cup of coffee."

"Ah, this is good coffee, Catchel," Tomas said lifting his cup to the owner of the Coffee shop. He'd loaded it with plenty of sugar and cinnamon. Catchel's coffee shop was in the corner of the market building in downtown Brownsville. It was the melting place in town.

"Thanks," Gabriel Catchel answered, "I'm glad you approve it. I heard that the Cortina brothers have joined the Separatist Movement. Is that right?"

"Yes," Answered Chema, "we must protect our rights to the land." His face reddened as he spoke. "Many of the newcomers are claiming that the land is there for whoever comes and takes possession of it."

"But, you are siding with Stillman, King and Kenedy, who are among those who are taking advantage of the difficult situation of many of the Mexicans."

"True," Cheno intervened, "but, first we must clear the validity of our titles. I realize that by doing that, it will also validate the land they have got thus far." He sipped his coffee. "Indeed, this is good coffee," he said smiling to Tomas, "A Commission is already reviewing the issue. They have started in Laredo and will be here soon. I'm hopeful that they will respect and make everybody respect the treaty signed in Guadalupe Hidalgo." His voice hardened. "Otherwise we must become independent."

"I hope it won't get to that point," Chema said. "I'm sure the

33

Commission will see the honesty of our claim. Otherwise, a lot of our people are running the risk of being ripped off by all of these lawyers."

"We'll not let it happen to us again. We'll defend our rights. But we must do it the legal way." Cheno replied. "For that reason we must become involved in politics to be sure that the candidates who are likely to be fair to Mexicans are elected."

"Speaking about that," Catchel intervened. "James Brown and Stephen Powers have been looking for you." He paused for a minute to make a sign to one of his employees to answer to the request for service of another customer, it was the busy hour and the place was buzzing. "Jaime wants you to help him to become Sheriff, and you know that Stephen is planning to run for Mayor and also wants your help."

"I would trust neither one of them," Tomas said. "They are gringos, and care only for other gringos. I, like almost everyone else, would like to see one of you in those positions."

Some of the customers overheard what Tomas had said and started clapping. Francisco Iturria and Jose San Roman, wealthy Mexican businessmen living in Brownsville, who were sitting at another table, looked at each other and shrugged their shoulders, in disdain.

"We all know that under the present circumstances what Tomas suggests isn't possible," Cheno said looking toward the table where Iturria and San Roman sat. "But, at least we should get together to be sure that we elect people who are fair not only to the wealthy Mexicans but also to the peons and vaqueros. We should look out not only for our business, but also for our people." He spoke loudly, being sure that everyone would listen.

"Cheno, you have been a rich landlord all of your life," Francisco Iturria said. "That has allowed you to waste years in the company of rough vaqueros, taming wild horses, hunting and fighting. But some of us have had to work hard for what we got. So, it will be better for us if we just make the best of the time, instead of dreaming. One earns respect by working and going along with the circumstances."

Jose San Roman nodded in agreement.

"Yes, we'll go along with the circumstances, but we won't tolerate circumstances that exploit and rob our friends. That's the main reason we joined the separatist movement." said Cheno, his voice raising. "And I hope that you will join us in defense of our rights."

"You do whatever you believe is right and we'll do the same." San Roman replied.

Stillman sat in his newly built office at Elizabeth Street and offered his guests cigars. "Gentlemen, we are here to prepare for the upcoming Sheriff's election." He pointed toward Henry Khan, a robust man whose ruddy cheeks showed how much he enjoyed whiskey. "We all have benefited during Henry's tenure as County Judge," Stillman continued, "so, now I'd like to propose him as our candidate for

County's Sheriff."

"We all owe him more than one favor," said Samuel Belden, "I certainly second and support his nomination."

"He has supported our business and is tough on low- class criminals. He's our best choice," said William Neale

"Does anyone oppose?" Stillman asked. He looked around the room. Not a man stirred or said a word. "It is agreed then, Henry Khan is our candidate for Sheriff." He smoked his cigar, taking a moment before continuing. "There might be some opposition from James Brown, but if we plan it well, he shouldn't give us much trouble."

"Cortina is becoming a nuisance for us," said Mifflin Kenedy, owner of the monopoly of steam boats on the river and Stillman's business partner. He looked at the men sitting in leather chairs. The smoke of cigars dimmed the evening light. "He is using his influence to elect those who won't support business. He believes, and is making other Mexicans believe, that they can become like us, real Americans." He grinned.

"We must make them understand that we won the war," Major Chapman intervened. "Sabas, like Pancho and Jose here," he said pointing toward the last two, understand it, and mind only their own business. But Cheno and Chema believe as you've said."

"For the time being we need the Cortina's in the separatist movement, but we must not allow them to gain power." Richard King, co owner of the steam boat monopoly, said.

"This is a moment of opportunity for all of us. Large amounts of land are becoming available for whoever wants to take it. Cattle also are easily available. But first we must control Mexicans who want to hold onto the land and people like Cortina who believes that because the Mexicans are in the majority they can have the control." Neale said.

"Adolphus and I have developed a plan that is already working," King intervened again. "It will help to control Cheno, but, before I go any further, we must have your acquiescence, since this is something in which all of us must agree."

"What is it?" Stillman asked. He moved nervously in his chair. I hope is a sensible plan, he thought.

"Adolphus, this is your idea, please explain," King said.

"Well," Glaevecke started as he wiped the sweat of his forehead with the back of his left hand. "It's simple; Cortina is leading a ring of cattle's thieves on both sides of the river."

"How do you know that?" Iturria asked. "We all know that he has no need to do anything like that."

"Well," Glaevecke responded, a cynical grin in his face, "he just took possession of fifty longhorns that the Garza's claim were stolen from their ranch in Mexico a couple of weeks ago."

"If that is true," Iturria said, "why the need for secrecy?" He also wiped the sweat from his forehead.

"We have tricked him well," King intervened again, "Cortina just bought the herd from Adolphus, now we must make the Garza family and everyone else, believe that Cortina is stealing cattle. Mifflin and I just recovered a couple of a hundred heads that Cortina had stolen from us." Glancing toward Kenedy, he asked. "Isn't that right Mifflin?"

Kenedy hesitated before agreeing.

"I don't like this," Iturria said, "I won't take part in this scheme."

"But, you will keep your mouth shut," Stillman said glaring at Iturria. He wanted to make sure the threat was clear. If Iturria crossed them, he'd pay.

"Yes, of course," Iturria answered meekly.

"Go ahead as you have planned," Stillman said to King and Glaevecke. "We'll support and help to spread your allegations." He turned around looking at all those present. "For the time being let's concentrate on getting Henry elected."

A couple of weeks later, at the newly built City Hall, around seventy men attended the caucus to elect the new Sheriff. Everybody was sweating profusely. Jars of homemade tamarindo, Jamaica flower and lemonade drinks along with tequila and zotol were available. The night sea breeze also helped to make the evening almost comfortable.

"As you know we are here to elect our new Sheriff," said Jerry Galvan -an Irishman and one of Stillman's business partner. He had lived in Matamoros for several years, and had changed his last name to give it a Hispanic sound. He was acting as leader for the caucus. "The candidates are well known to all of us. Henry Khan, please stand," he said pointing to where Khan sat. Khan stood up smiling and raising his right hand. "And James Brown," Galvan continued pointing to Brown, who also stood and waived to those present. "Would anyone like to say something before we proceed with the election?"

"Yes," said Samuel Belden standing. "We all know that Henry," pointing to Khan, "is the best man for the job. He is tough with criminals, and during his tenure as County Judge, business improved."

"Tough with Mexicans peons and good for Stillman's business," a voice in the back said

Stillman made a signal to Glaevecke who nodded toward two men standing near the entrance. They started toward the location of the voice.

"Mr. Chairman," William Neale, an English man and owner of a stage coach from Point Isabel, in the seacoast, to Brownsville, and also Stillman's business partner, said. "We all know both candidates well. I move we proceed with the election."

At that moment Stillman heard the sounds of horses approaching.

"Does anyone else wish to speak before we proceed?" Galvan asked.

"Yes, I have something to say," a powerful voice came from the back of the room.

"Who is that? Will you please come forward?" Galvan asked.

"Juan Nepomuceno Cortina Goseascochea," Cheno said as he approached, his boots leaving a trail of mud. Sixty Mexicans entered the room behind him.

. Stillman's men stood up. Tension filled the air.

"Friends," Cheno began, as soon as he was facing the assembly, his voice was clear and powerful. "We are here to elect our next Sheriff. We need to choose someone who is tough on criminals but also fair to all of us. Fair to the rich and powerful, but especially fair to the poor vaqueros, peons and peasants. The man who has proven to be that kind of person is our good friend Jaime." Cheno pointed to Brown who stood up smiling and waiving his right hand. Cheers and wild yells greeted him. "Now we can proceed with the election," Cheno said to Galvan, showing his white teeth.

James Brown was elected by overwhelming majority. Most of those present yelled happily when the results were announced.

"Viva Cheno Cortinas," a voice shouted. Stillman and his men left, obviously upset.

A Mexican let a savage cry go that was echoed by many more. Cheno smiled and joined with a long, wild, cry of his own.

CHAPTER 6

Jesus Sandoval had just finished collecting the eggs. He checked that the cows and horses had enough hay and walked toward his humble shack. His wife and children were already home. The smoking chimney signaled that dinner was almost ready. In the haziness of the late evening, he still could see the houses in Brownsville. Jesus smiled, life was good to him.

He had just been appointed assistant to the city Marshal. His small ranch produced enough and to top it all, Mr. King had just hired him to assist in the protection of his ranch. Now he could support his young wife and children. Arriving home, he kissed his wife Maria and the children Chuyito and Josefa. Satisfied, he sat at the table, ready for dinner.

"It has been good for us since the Americans came," he said to his wife, "I'd rather work for them than for those arrogant Mexicans landowners. Mr. King and Mr. Kenedy are scaring the Mexicans away and that's good. I'm happy to help them." Then he looked at her smiling. "They call me Cassoos, but I don't mind."

Several strange sounds caught his attention; they seemed to come from a short distance away. It was like a combination of animal sounds, the hissing of a snake and the growl of dogs. The burst of noises came in rapid sequence. Jesus stood up and reached for his rifle, but before he could get to it, the front door was kicked open and a couple of Mezcalero Apache burst in. When Jesus turned to shoot something struck him on the head. The last thing he heard was Chuyito crying for his help.

He had no idea how long he might have been unconscious. By the time he opened his eyes, he was alone. His wife and children and almost all of his animals were gone. "Maria, Chuy, Josefa," he cried, to no avail. Staggering out he continued searching for them.

From a distance, he could see a group of men coming from Brownsville, galloping toward him. As they approached Jesus recognized Cheno Cortina, Antonio Tijerina and Sheriff Brown among them.

"We heard the cry of the Apache. What happened, Chucho?" Tijerina asked when the group stopped in front of his house.

Jesus explained to them what happened and asked for their help to recover his wife and children.

"They can't be far from here," Cheno said. "We can catch them if

38

we leave now."

"But it is already dark and they know the territory better than we do." Marshal Shears objected. "Besides, this is a job for the Army. I suggest that we wait until tomorrow and let the Army do something about it."

"We have no time to waste, if we don't act now, they will sell the children into slavery to other tribes or worse, sell them to the Comancheros," Cheno said. "Those of you, who are not afraid, join me. We must get to them tonight."

"I'm in," Tijerina said.

"You know I'll always follow you," Tomas Cabrera said. Sheriff Brown and the rest of the men, except for Shears and two others, agreed to pursue the Apache.

The night was unusually dark. The sudden flashes of an electric storm and the distant howling coyote caused goose bumps to crawl up Cheno's arms. It was almost midnight by the time they approached the Apache camp. Cheno felt his heart beating faster. I hope we are on time, he thought.

"Let's be silent," Cheno whispered. They dismounted and started walking carefully toward the Apache camp.

Cheno noticed that the Apache had chosen a bend in the Rio Grande for their camp that seemed ideal for their defense, almost completely surrounded by the river with only one way to get in or out. Fortunately for Cheno and his men, this fact made the Mezcalero careless. They had left only one on guard, and he appeared to be asleep on his feet.

Cheno, Antonio Tijerina, Jesus, Tomas Cabrera and the rest of the men approached slowly on foot. Cheno signaled for them to divide in two groups, so they could prevent the Apache from escape. Once they were close enough, Cheno signaled for everybody to crawl the last few yards on their bellies. Slowly, and silently, they edged toward the entrance of the camp.

As they approached, Cheno became aware of Jesus, beside him, shaking, teeth clenched, eyes about to burst. Cheno realized that Jesus could no longer contain himself. Before Cheno could act, Jesus jumped up, knife in hand. With a savage yell, Jesus attacked the guard, slicing his throat with such skill that his head fell on his chest without making a sound. But Jesus' piercing cry alerted the sleeping Apaches. Startled to their feet, they immediately spotted their attackers.

It was a merciless fight. Each group knew that if defeated, there would be no survivors. Seeing that they were attacked from two sides, the Apache tried to retreat, but, their defensive location was now, inescapable. Some of the Apaches attempted to rush toward the river using their prisoners as shields, but it was to no avail, those who ran into the river drowned, the rest were killed.

With the Apache defeated, Jesus, Cheno, Tomas, Tijerina and the rest of the survivors, went looking for Jesus' wife and children. They found them in the arms of a dead mezcalero Apache, their throats slit wide open. When Jesus saw them, he cried so loud that it caused a cold chill to go up Cheno's back. Although, they all were used to violence, Cheno noticed that some of the men had tears in their eyes.

"Chucho," Tomas said touching Jesus' shoulder.

"Leave me alone," Jesus said, moving his shoulder away from Tomas. "I'll never forgive what you have done," he added with rancor in his voice. "From now on, all Indians, all Mexicans are my enemies. I'll make them pay for what you have done to me, to my family." He looked around. His naturally black eyes, swollen by the tears and blood, looked menacing. "Someday I'll take revenge against my enemies." He added, this time staring at Tomas.

"Chucho, you are confused and in pain," Tijerina intervened. "We are your friends. We have known each other for many years." He extended his hand toward Jesus Sandoval who spit on it, as he jumped back.

"Cabrones," Jesus screamed, "you are not my friends, you never have been. I despise you and you and you, I despise all of you, and I always have. But now, I have no reasons to pretend otherwise." His face was reddened and swollen, and foam streamed from his lips. "I'll take revenge, you will see, to me you are nothing but pigs."

"God and time will show you how wrong you are," Cheno said. "We are sorry for what has happened to your family. If you want, we can help you, take them to the cemetery, so they can have a Christian burial and rest in peace."

"Rest in peace?" Jesus screamed. He laughed hysterically.... a hard, loud, painful laugh. Suddenly he stopped. "Leave me alone," he screamed, "leave me alone before I kill you all."

A Mexican boy raced through the muddy streets of Brownsville. He ran so fast that he lost one of his huaraches. Scooping it up, he flew on until he stopped at the newly built brick house of Charles Stillman on Washington Street. "Senor Stillman, Senor Stillman," the Mexican boy yelled, banging on the solid wood door. "Senor Stillman, Senor Stillman!"

"What is it? Why are you banging on my door in that way?" Stillman asked as he opened the door, buttoning his shirt, his hair in disarray.

"The store, Senor Stillman, the store has been robbed," the boy answered breathlessly. "Senor Belden has sent me to inform you."

"What?" Stillman screamed. "What happened?"

"I don't know," the boy answered. "Senor Belden opened the store, and then asked me to run and tell you that the store has been robbed."

Stillman looked at the boy, frowned, passed his hand over his forehead. "Go and tell Samuel that I'll be there as soon as possible. And be sure you put that huarache on." He gave the boy a penny. Whoever did this, will pay dearly, Stillman thought as he closed the door.

It took him less than five minute to gallop to the store in Elizabeth Street. Stillman pushed through the crowd that had gathered outside and walked through the open front door. "Well, Samuel, what is missing?" he asked Belden.

"They took the forty-five Remington rifles that just arrived from New Orleans, fifty boxes of ammunition, twelve bags of flour, nineteen bags of salt and fifteen bags of nails," Belden answered.

Stillman looked at the hole in the ceiling and the rope hanging from it. "Marshall, do you have any idea about who might have done this?" Stillman asked Shears who had got there earlier.

"Juan Contreras saw a couple of Mexicans coming out of the store. He recognized one of them, from a ranch nearby," Shears answered. "We'll go and start questioning the people there. As you know, Mexicans are hard and protect each other." Then he grinned. "But, I'm taking Cassoos Sandoval with me. He knows how to make people speak fast."

"Good," Stillman said, a serious look in his face. "I expect results soon."

A few hours later, at a small ranch nearby, Marshal Shears, Jesus Sandoval, William Neale and others ravaged the few shacks there. All of the grown men, teen age males and most of the women were flogged. Most of them knew nothing; a few said that five men had ties with bandoleros. Sandoval passed a lasso around the neck of these men. Another lasso, bound their ankles. The ends of both lassos were tied to horses' neck. Jesus Sandoval skillfully controlled the horses so the men's bodies were under tension. The ropes held them on the air by their necks and feet, causing severe pain and almost separating their heads from the body. This method bore results quickly.

They said that those who did the robbery were from El Ranchito, a small town, just across the river. Their leader was Juan Chapa. The robbers had stopped at their ranch to water their horses and had bragged about having robbed one of the gringos who had been robbing Mexicans. As soon as Sandoval had the information, he let the horses pull apart as much as they could, for the hanging men the pain was unbearable, but short. The mosquitos feasted on their blood. Letting the living to take care of the dead, Shears, Sandoval, Neale and the rest mounted and galloped back to Brownsville.

"Juan Chapa, eh?" Stillman asked Shears, rubbing his chin. "From El Ranchito, I've been there," he mumbled. "But, are you sure?"

"Cassoos method of interrogation is flawless," Shears answered a cynical smile in his face.

"Well, you and your men must go there. You will show them that they can't come and rob us and not be punished. Bring this Juan Chapa to me, preferably alive, "Stillman said, "and take this Cassoos with you. He seems to be a useful man," he added after a moment's thought.

A couple of days later the little village of El Ranchito was burning, anything that moved was shot. Shears and his men made sure that the only man kept alive was Juan Chapa, who was beaten and taken to Brownsville.

"So, this is Juan Chapa, the man who thought he could steal from me, eh," Stillman said with a grin, when the badly injured Chapa was presented to him.

"No, senor, I don't know what you are talking about," Juan Chapa answered, crying. "Please believe me, I never stole from you or anyone else, I'm an honest farmer. All that I want is to live in peace, please, believe me." He added sobbing like a child.

"Who are your compadres?" Shears screamed at Chapa, kicking him. "Who was with you? We'll teach all of you a lesson. Come on, talk."

"Senor, I have told you a thousand times. I know nothing about any stealing." Chapa answered.

"What's your name?" Stillman asked.

"Juan Chapa Guerra," Chapa answered.

"A whole town has accused you. It will be better for you to tell us the truth and identify your accomplices. If you do so, I'll be merciful with you." Stillman said.

Chapa threw himself at Stillman's feet, "Please, Senor, believe me, please, I don't know anything."

"It's your choice," Stillman said coldly, moving away from Chapa. "Cassoos will question him, now," he said to Shears before leaving.

Two weeks later, Marshal Shears presented himself at Stillman's store. He was frowning. He looked deeply concerned. "May I talk to Mr. Stillman?" he asked the clerk. The clerk went inside the office, then came back and showed Shears the way in.

"Mr. Stillman, I have important news that concerns you." Shears said, hesitant, "but, maybe I should wait until you are alone."

"Nonsense, William and the Reverend Chamberlain are people I trust." Stillman pointed to William Neale and Reverend Hiram Chamberlain, who were there on business.

"Well," Shears said not sure how to start.

"Come on, say what you have to say, we don't have time to waste." Stillman said impatiently.

"A man was captured in Monterrey. He was selling Remington rifles and ammunition," Shears said. "He was arrested because he got drunk and killed a man." He hesitated.

"So?" Stillman shrugged.

"The name of the man was Juan Chapa Garcia. He told the Mexican authorities that the goods he was trying to sell were stolen from you," Shears said almost apologetically, "it seems that we killed an innocent man."

"Mexicans are liars, they are an insolent and inferior race," Reverend Chamberlain intervened. "You have taught then a lesson they won't forget."

Neale nodded in agreement.

Stillman rubbed his chin as he did every time that he was concerned.

"Word of this is spreading fast," Shears said. "Already there are some Mexicans, Iturria and San Roman among them, manifesting concern."

"Do you remember Somerville?" Stillman asked Shears.

"That's the man who was killed and robbed some time ago by Juan de la Luna." Shears nodded "Why do you ask?"

"Glaevecke claimed that this man, de la Luna, knew Cortina, and that Cortina was the one who sold the mules to Somerville. Well, it's time for the people to know about this, and about the cattle stolen from Garza." Stillman replied.

Tomas along with Atanasio and other vaqueros were looking for several lost cows at Cheno's ranch. The noon sun was ablaze, the air was thick with moisture, and there were no clouds in the blue sky. Both, men and horses were sweating heavily. The men's cotton shirts clung to their skin; their lips were dry as they guided the longhorns back to the ranch. Mosquitoes were buzzing all around them. Tomas had felt an ill-defined discomfort since the Sandoval event. Now, he felt nauseated, a cold chill gripping his entire body, he felt upset by the shivering of his body. He turned to get a sarape to cover himself when suddenly; he fell from his pinto, shaking and vomiting, a black, foul-smelling vomit.

Atanasio and the rest of the men took him back to his jacal. One of them went to notify Cheno, who was supervising the branding of recently tamed colts. As soon as Cheno heard the news about Tomas he ran to his friend's bedside.

Here, we go again, the black vomit is back, Cheno was thinking as he galloped on his horse. Why does God punish us with this disease? He asked himself. El vomito negro killed my mother's first husband and later my own father, and now Tomas. But Tomas is strong. Since my father died; he has taken care of my brothers and me. Now, it seems that it is the time we take care of him, but what can we do?

Cheno entered Tomas' shack. Coming from noon brightness, Cheno had some difficulty finding his way in the darkness of the place. The only window was covered by a blanket. Cheno's spurs left a trail in the clean dirt floor. Tomas lay on his bed, sweating profusely, and breathing with difficulty.

"Tomas, viejo, how are feeling?" Cheno asked as soon as he was at his bedside.

"How do you think?" Tomas answered, with a smile interrupted as he suddenly shivered and vomited. Cheno went for a rag, held Tomas' head and gently cleansed his mouth. Tomas smiled revealing his black- stained teeth. "Don't you worry," he said to Cheno, "I'm like the mesquite, I have deep roots."

Estefana and Rafaela entered the shack. "We need more light in here," Estefana said, pulling the blanket away from the window. "There are many others who are also sick. They all will need care. We'll organize the women to nurse them, the least we can do is to protect them from being stung by mosquitos." She added as she took a cotton blanket and used it to create a shield around Tomas.

"We'll need lots of fresh water. Cheno, please be sure that the aguadores deliver plenty of fresh water here," Rafaela said

The sound of galloping horses approaching called their attention.

"Where is Cortina?" somebody asked in a harsh voice as soon as they got close. Seconds later Marshal Shears, Sheriff Brown and several other men entered the shack.

"Juan Nepomuceno Cortina," Shears said as soon as he saw Cheno, "you are accused of cattle rustling and indicted for the murder and robbery of John Somerville."

"What?" Estefana asked, "Who has accused my son of such crimes?"

"He has committed no crime, I can swear to that," Tomas said trying to get up, but falling in bed again.

Rafaela seized Cheno's arm.

"Adolphus Glaevecke has signed a statement to Judge Watrous," Shears continued, "I have an order for your arrest."

"I'm going nowhere," Cheno replied, "I'll present myself to Judge Watrous as soon as I'm sure people in my ranch with black vomit are cared for."

By then, the word of Cheno's indictment had spread and Cheno's men had surrounded Tomas' jacal.

"I trust Cheno's word," Sheriff Brown said. "He'll come whenever Judge Watrous asks him to be present in court."

Shears hesitated, but one of his men whispered to his ear that they were surrounded. "Well, Cortinas you have been notified, present yourself to Judge Watrous as soon as possible."

"I'll be there," Cheno replied.

CHAPTER 7

For weeks, Tomas suffered fever, nausea, vomiting. He lost weigh and although he was slender, the black vomit got him to his bare bones. The rough vaquero life had made him strong and the gentle weather of early fall came to his aid; so, unlike hundreds of less fortunate souls he survived the epidemics.

"Viejo, I'm happy to see that you are as tough as the mesquite tree," Cheno said smiling during a visit to his recovering friend.

"You know the old saying: 'crabgrass never dies'" Tomas replied, laughing. "But, talking seriously, everyone here is thankful for what Dona Estefana and Rafaela have done for the sick people." Pushing himself up, he continued, "I don't know what they did, but I know that without their help, things could have been worse."

Cheno noticed that his teeth were still stained with black. Tomas' face became troubled; the creases on his face looked deeper as he continued. "But now you must solve a more serious problem. You are accused of cattle rustling and murder by that rascal of your cousin. If you want, I could arrange for him to meet the devil."

"That won't be necessary, I can prove my innocence. But I'll never forgive that rascal as you righteously called him." Cheno frowned and paced around; as he did he lifted a bit of dust from the earthen floor. "There are others, more powerful than him, who want to put me down. They know that the accusations are false," Cheno said. He stopped sitting in a palm chair. "Adolphus is their lackey. They want to plant the seed of suspicion on my intentions, so others won't support the effort to defend our rights against their greed." His face saddened. His voice trembled as he spoke. "Even Sabas has told me that he believes the accusations." He rested his chin on his chest, rubbing his beard, pensive. He didn't want Tomas to notice that a tear was welling up.

"Sabas is ambitious, always has been," Tomas said, his hand on Cheno's shoulder, "but he is a good man and a Mexican and above all, he is your brother. I can't image him turning his back on you. I'm sure he'll support you when the time comes."

"I hope you are right, but he has always sided with those he calls 'our class'," Cheno replied. "As you well know, he has never approved that Chema and I party with you or the other vaqueros. He has always criticized my choice of friends." Cheno stood up. "Well, it's time for me to leave." He grinned. "Chema has agreed to take my defense in the upcoming hearing with Judge Watrous. As you know, he is the learned one in the family. Well, take care and don't try to do too much, you are still weak, and we need you in good shape." He added, as he gave his friend a gentle slap on the shoulder and walked toward the door. His spurs raised dust, leaving a trail as he exited.

One week later Cheno and Chema sat in Judge Watrous court, on the second floor of the newly built market building. Cheno noticed that all available seats were taken. Dona Estefana, Rafaela and Sabas, were among those present. Also, Stillman, Kenedy, Iturria, San Roman, Neale and other prominent businessmen were there. Cheno smiled when he noticed that the majority was common people, peons and vaqueros, most of his friends were there.

"Mr. Glaevecke," said Judge Watrous, a tall, robust man with large blue eyes and a square jaw. He was impressive with his dark robe, sitting in his high bench. "You have accused Mr. Cortina of two crimes. One is for the murder of Mr. John Somerville from Kentucky." He looked straight down to Adolphus Glaevacke who, sitting at the witness stand, looked chubbier and shorter from where Cheno was sitting.

"The other charge is for rustling cattle from a Mr. Salvador de la Garza from Matamoros, Mexico. We'll see first the accusation for murder. Are you able to provide this court with proof that this crime was committed by Mr. Cortina?"

"Your honor," Glaevecke answered. "The mules stolen from Mr. Somerville were sold by Juan Nepomuceno Cortina. He has always been friendly to rough and lawless men. Juan De la Luna worked as a vaquero at El Carmen ranch, which belongs to Dona Estefana Cortina, mother of the accused. Juan de la Luna and Cortina were seen together at many saraos in Matamoros. De la Luna was hired as a guide for Mr. Somerville. De la Luna killed Somerville and stole the mules under orders by Juan Nepomuceno Cortina."

"We are not here to judge the friends of Mr. Cortina," Judge Watrous said. "Do you have any evidence that Mr. Cortina was a member of Mr. Somerville party?"

"Well, no, your honor."

"Is there any evidence that Mr. Cortina was at the place where the crime was committed?"

"No, your honor," Glaevecke answered. "As I said, Juan de la Luna murdered Mr. Somerville by order of Juan Cortina, to recover his mules."

"Do you or anyone else, have evidence that the stolen mules came back to Mr. Cortina?"

"Well, as I said," Glaevecke mumbled hesitantly.

"Show us the evidence," Judge Watrous said in a harsh voice, staring at Glaevecke.

"Well, your Honor, everybody knows about Cortina's friendship with De la Luna," Glaevecke answered meekly.

"Marshall Shears, do you have any other witnesses, who could help to clarify the murder of Mr. Somerville?" Judge Watrous asked Shears his blue eyes piercing him.

"No, your Honor, Mr. Glaevecke is the only person who has come forward," the Marshall answered. "But, in my opinion…"

"If I become interested in your opinion, I'll ask for it," Judge Watrous interrupted Shears, while turning to face Cheno and Jose Maria, who were sitting on the bench reserved for the defendant. "Is there anything you want to say in your defense?" the Judge asked.

"Yes, your Honor," Jose Maria replied, "I'm Jose Maria Cortina Goseascochea, and I'm representing the defendant Juan Nepomuceno Cortina Goseascochea." He stood up and faced the Judge.

"I suppose that's agreeable with you," the Judge said to Cheno.

"Yes, your Honor." Cheno answered, standing up.

"Well, let's listen," the Judge said passing his left hand over his face then making a cup with the palm of his hand to hold his chin, his elbow resting on the desk, facing Chema.

"Besides the fact that my brother sold the mules to Mr. Somerville, there is no evidence that they mingled in any other way. He wasn't among Mr. Somerville's party of guides to Durango," Jose Maria began. "Juan Nepomuceno Cortina never saw Mr. Somerville again. The mules never went back to El Carmen ranch and Juan de la Luna never came back to join our mother's ranch," Jose Maria stood up. "At the time the murder was committed my brother was out catching and taming wild horses. There are several vaqueros who will testify to that, if necessary. However, considering that only Mr. Glaevecke accuses my brother, and he can't show any evidence to support his word. I ask your Honor to dismiss the charges against my brother."

"That's right," someone from the crowd yelled, while others clapped. Cheno looked at his brother with pride.

Judge Watrous hit the bench with his gavel. "The audience will remain silent," he said. "Otherwise I'll order to clear the court." He stared at Chema for a moment. Then, he turned to face Glaevecke. "Mr. Glaevecke, I ask you again. Do you have any proof of your accusation against Mr. Cortina?"

"As I said your Honor," Glaevecke answered, swallowing saliva. "Everyone knows that Juan de la Luna is a friend of Cheno Cortina. Everybody knows that all the low- class vaqueros and peons see Cheno Cortina as their leader. I saw Juan de la Luna talking to Cortina just before Somerville's party left town. Somerville was found death shortly afterwards. I believe Juan de la Luna murdered Somerville under orders of Cheno Cortina."

"So, your belief is the only evidence you can provide to this court," Judge Watrous said. "That makes it easy for me to rule in this case. The charge of murder against Mr. Juan Nepomuceno Cortina is hereby dismissed." Most in the room clapped and cheered. Cheno noticed that Stillman grinned as he whispered something in Kenedy's ears.

Judge Watrous turned and faced Marshal Shears. "I hope that you have better witnesses in the charge of cattle rustling," he said in a harsh voice.

"Yes, your Honor. Here is Mr. Salvador De la Garza, from Matamoros," Shears answered.

Salvador De la Garza, a tall, slender man, with gray hair and a thick, also gray, moustache walked toward the witness stand. His short, Mexican style, boots made a sharp sound as he walked toward the witness stand. Cheno smiled. He'd known De la Garza since he was a child. Both had the same roots.

"Mr. De la Garza. Welcome. Do you understand English?" Judge Watrous asked.

"Un poquito," De la Garza answered.

"Well. If you prefer to give testimony in Spanish there is a translator available," Judge Watrous said as he lifted a glass of water and drank a bit.

De la Garza nodded. The translator, a petite woman with short black hair, walked and stood by his side, facing the Judge.

"Mr. De la Garza," Judge Watrous continued. "What do you have to say to this court?"

"One hundred and fifty longhorns were stolen from my ranch, just across the river," De la Garza said in Spanish. "Fifty of them were found at Mr. Cortinas's ranch."

"How do you know that they are your cattle?" Judge Watrous asked.

"They have my brand," De la Garza answered.

Judge Watrous turned and faced Cheno and Chema. "What do you have to say to that?"

"Your Honor," Chema stood up. "Mr. Cortinas bought those longhorns from Mr. Glaevecke in the honest belief that Mr. De la Garza had sold them to him. If somebody is to blame of cattle rustling, there is you man." Chema pointed to Glaevecke.

Judge Watrous turned toward the witness. "Mr. De la Garza, you say that fifty heads of the stolen cattle are in possession of Mr. Cortina. But you also say that one hundred and fifty longhorns were stolen from you. Do you know where the other one hundred are?"

"Well, you Honor," De la Garza answered, after a moment of hesitation, "apparently some of them were seen at Santa Gertrudis and Los Laureles ranches. But, the brand has been visibly altered."

"Are you accusing Mr. King, or Mr. Kenedy?" Judge Watrous asked.

"The brand has been changed. It would be hard for me to prove anything. So I accuse no one." De la Garza replied.

"But you are accusing Mr. Cortina." Marshal Shears intervened.

"Marshal," Judge Watrous shouted. "I already told you that if I need your opinion, I'll ask for it."

"I apologize, your Honor," Shears replied.

"Please continue," Judge Watrous said to De la Garza.

"As I said," De la Garza continued. "I accuse no one. I've known Cheno Cortina for many years. He is a great vaquero. Rough and a bit wild, but honest. He has no need to steal cattle." De la Garza frowned and raised his voice. "There are hundreds of longhorns roaming in our range lands. In the past they were there for whoever caught and branded them. But now, a few men have taken all as their own and not happy with that. They take other people's cattle and hire gunmen to protect them." He turned and faced Cheno. "I believe Cortina when he says that he bought the cattle in good faith. All that I ask is to have my cattle returned to me."

"The charges of cattle rustling against Juan Nepomuceno Cortina are hereby dismissed. As long as the cattle are returned to its rightful owner," Judge Watrous said slamming the bench with his gavel. "We'll deal with Mr. Adolphus Glaevecke for buying and selling stolen cattle later." He turned and faced Shears. "Marshal I'll see you in my quarters."

Estefana and Rafaela hugged each other. Most of the present cheered and clapped.

Stillman went and shook hands with Cheno. "Congratulations, you got off and I hope you won't have any more trouble," he said smiling.

"Thank you," Cheno answered. "I hope we'll learn to respect each other and live in peace."

Two weeks later, Cheno serenaded Rafaela outside her bedroom window at her home in Matamoros. After the serenade, they talked through the bars of her window. Cheno noticed that Rafaela, although obviously happy, seemed distressed. "What's wrong?" he asked. "What's bothering you?"

"Cheno, I'm worried. Ugly things are happening on both sides of the border," she answered. "This morning in Brownsville, as I was shopping in the market, two drunken men were making a lot of noise. They seemed to be having a good time. Although noisy, they bothered nobody. As a matter of fact, most present seemed to be enjoying their jokes," her voice trembled as she continued. "Then Marshal Shears came, with his ugly mastiff," she sobbed squeezing Cheno's hand.

"Come, come," he said, holding both of her hands, "relax now and tell me what happened."

"Oh, Cheno, how can anyone be so cruel?" she said still sobbing.

Cheno said nothing. He just held her hands gently, waiting for her to continue.

"Marshal Shears, unleashed the mastiff," she continued after a few seconds. "One of them caught one of the men at his throat and would have killed him if it had not been for one of the onlookers who kicked the dog away from the man." Her face now reddened. Her beautiful black eyes shone as the tears rolled down her cheeks. "But not happy with it, Marshal Shears had both men stripped and whipped them so violently that both of their backs were severely slashed, blood bursting from their wounds. 'This is to teach you all, no lawless drunk will be allowed in my town,' he said." She calmed down, looking at Cheno.

"He has gone too far," he said. "Someone must put a stop to his abuse." He looked at Rafaela. "But, you said that something else happened here, in Matamoros."

"Oh, yes," she smiled. "Although not as bad, it is embarrassing. This afternoon, as I left the ferry, I saw a woman, dressed as a man, her hair cut short, in tears, riding a white donkey." She stared at Cheno. He felt intrigued and smiled back at her.

"Who was she? Why was she punished in that way?" he asked.

"Well," she answered. "I asked the same question to my uncle. He told me that she is Susana Gomez, wife of Captain Gomez, who was expelled by General Woll because of his liberal ideas. She was caught distributing copies of El Rayo Federal, the newspaper that liberals are now printing in Brownsville. General Woll ordered that she be dressed as a man, her hair cut and taken around town on a white donkey 'for daring to barge into the male sphere of political activism.' Now, that is humiliating and upsetting."

Cheno laughed. "El General de los calzones colorados (General red under underpants) at action again. Don't let that upset you my dear. Conservatives will be out of power soon," he said holding her hands gently, caressing her with his eyes. "We have more important things of our own to talk about. We should start talking about the wedding," he said as he showed her a beautiful gold ring. "I bought it from a French Captain at Bagdad. He told me that this ring comes from a place called Venice, in Europe."

"Oh, Cheno," Rafaela said visibly excited. "Are you sure? Are you ready?"

"Yes, of course," Cheno answered. "You know very well, that I was waiting only for the ranch to become productive. In spite of the problem with the stolen cattle that I was fool enough to buy from Adolphus, the ranch is doing very well. I'll talk to your parents next week, I guess they are already expecting it and I have taken the liberty to talk to father Nicolas. He has agreed to marry us in the Cathedral." Cheno noticed that Rafaela was listening with an ecstatic expression. He felt happy.

"But, there is so much to plan," she said.

"Yes, I know," Cheno replied. "You'll take care of that." Cheno noticed that Rafaela's face showed sudden distress.

"Cheno, I'm afraid of Marshal Shears. He has become your sworn enemy." She held Cheno's hands. "He is ruthless and won't stop at anything to harm you. And you know that he has the support of important people."

"No need to worry. It's true that there are powerful men in both sides of the river who are against me," Cheno said confidently. "But, both Brownsville Mayor and the Sheriff owe their election to me. With their help Chema will be elected the County's Tax Assessor and Collector." He smiled proudly. "They are learning to respect us." He caressed Rafaela's cheeks tenderly. "This is our moment. Start planning the wedding."

CHAPTER 8

"Cheno, I'm happy that you have asked for Rafaela's hand. For generations our families have grown together. I'm proud to have you as my son in law." Felix Cortez, Rafaela's father, said.

"As I'm honored to become part of your family," Cheno said.

Felix Cortez nodded with pleasure. "I agree with the idea that, after the wedding, you and Rafaela will live in the northern side of the border. Here, the high tariff on customs imposed by General Woll and the conservatives has made business almost not profitable." He sipped his coffee with cinnamon. "Smuggling has increased more than ever. It is profitable for those who have the means to transport the goods through the river, all the way to Roma and from there, to Monterrey."

"Yes, Stillman, King, Kenedy and those who have moved their business to Brownsville and control the transport through the river are making a fortune," Cheno replied. "But even some Mexicans like Iturria, San Roman and my own family are doing well." He rocked in the bejuco chair, feeling comfortable in the living room of his future father in law. "The Americans are content with letting us share with their business. But they want us away from political positions of some importance." Cheno smoked his cigar and smiled, "on the good side of it." he continued, "most of the population in the Rio Grande valley is Mexican. If we become organized and vote, we'll have the upper hand."

"Be careful, even among Mexicans, there are many who consider you wild and dangerous," Felix said, then he paused for a moment, pensive. "Perhaps, you should be like Sabas, who minds only about his own business." He paused again, a concerned look on his face. "The Americans won't let you, or anyone of us, to get the upper hand in politics. If you are good to them, they might let you share a crumb, but, that's it." He sipped his coffee and stared at Cheno. "I must tell you this," he continued. "I don't want Rafaela to suffer. Mind your own business and let others worry about the fate of the underdogs."

Cheno sipped his coffee, smoked his cigar, rocking slowly in the chair. "Don't worry, Don Felix," he said. "I know how to take care of myself. Also, I'll take good care of Rafaela." He stared back at Felix. "I'll protect her. But you well know that if we remain passive, minding our own business, as you say, they won't change their methods and we'll be third class citizens in what, just a short time ago, used to be our country."

"You are a good man and I admire your courage, but once again, be careful. You have many friends in both sides of the border. But, also, many enemies," Felix said. He sighed. Extending his right hand he touched Cheno in the shoulder. "Take care, son. Glaevecke and Shears won't forgive the embarrassment that you caused them. They will do anything to harm you."

"Thank you, Don Felix," Cheno said holding Felix's hand. "I'll be careful and I promise to take good care of Rafaela."

"Well, enough of that," Felix said, slapping his right thigh. "How would you like some tamales for breakfast? Rafaela and your future mother in law just prepared them."

"Delighted," Cheno said, smiling. They got up, crossed the interior patio and walked to the dining room.

That night, Tomas Cabrera joined a group of Mexicans at Pedro's Tijerina ranch.

"Violence and humiliation to us has reached intolerable levels," Pedro Tijerina said to them. Among those present Tomas recognized Dionaciano Cantu, Lazaro Garza, Inocencio Flores and others who had participated in the resistance movement.

"Kenedy, Stillman, King, through their lackeys, are forcing many to sell at ridiculous prices," Tijerina continued as he paced the wooded floor of the room. "These are difficult times for us. It is not only our land that is being taken away, but also our pride and dignity." He stopped. "But what can we do?" He sat and passed his right hand over his forehead, a sad look in his face.

Tomas sensed impotence and a hint of desperation in the group. "We still have pride and dignity. We must defend our rights by any necessary means," he said.

"Whether we like it or not, we were defeated and this land is now part of Texas," Dionaciano Cantu intervened. "We must accept that our way of life has changed. Stillman and the others are taking advantage of our ignorance of the new law. Maybe we should try to learn it and use it to defend ourselves."

Everyone laughed.

"The law is only for the use of gringos," Lazaro Garza replied. "Two months ago I went to Austin planning to show proof of ownership." He stared at the men around him, his lower lip quivering. "Before I could say anything I was told that I would need two white men to swear that I'm a trustworthy person." His voice shook. His right hand closed in a fist. "I'd rather lose all of my land before I accept such humiliation." He slapped at the table in front of him. "Worse," he continued, "that even applies to those who fought among them for Texas independence."

"Billy Neale killed two young Mexicans in broad day light because they serenaded Antonieta Morales." Atanasio Flores intervened. "She has rejected his advances and is afraid of him. Still he walks the streets like no wrong was ever done. The law? Ha, it only protects them. If they could, they would kill all of l us." He spit on the floor and kicked a chair.

"Another example, well known to everyone is Steve Morris and the professional gamblers at the saloons, "Severo Morales said "They have killed several Mexicans over gambling disputes. They're still around cheating Mexicans, but if one of us gets drunk, he is severely punished. Cattle are stolen from us every day. But, if a Mexican is caught stealing, he is killed on the spot." He looked around. "But, as Pedro said, what can we do?"

"We fight back by any necessary means," Tomas intervened again.

"Come on, Tomas," Tijerina snapped. "Even your patron seems to have been tamed."

"No, you are wrong," Tomas replied. "Cheno is on our side. He is trying to get us organized and gain control through politics."

"Bah, politics is a waste of time. The gringos won't let us take any important position," Tijerina said. "However, we must admit that he was successful in electing Brown as Sheriff and has good chances in getting Chema elected as Tax assessor/collector. Those are steps in the right direction." He looked around to all the present. "What do you think?"

"Mexicans have been killed and their assassins are still free," Dionaciano Cantu said. "The man that people respect and consider their leader is playing politics." He frowned, "but, for the time being we don't seem to have another choice."

"I agree," Lazaro Garza said. "But remember, Cheno helped Stephen Powers to get elected as Brownsville's Mayor and in spite of that, Powers has become King's legal weapon. Mexicans are forced to sell or else. Besides trying politics, we should get ready for the use of force, if that becomes necessary."

"I hope it won't be necessary," Tijerina said. "In any case, I agree. We should be ready. Lazaro and Tomas will be in charge of getting our men organized."

That same night, at Brownsville, Cheno, Sabas and Chema had dinner at the elegant Barrate's restaurant, at the corner of Elizabeth and 13th Street. Sabas had connected with a group of Cubans who were interested in buying cattle in large number to be taken to their country. During dinner, they reached an agreement where Sabas and Estefana would provide 400 cattle and Cheno and Jose Maria would provide 200 cattle each. The cattle had to be delivered at Bagdad port in the Mexican side of the river, where the Cubans would have a boat waiting for them. It was a good deal and after dinner, the three brothers were in high spirits.

"What about going to King's place and having a little fun?" Cheno asked.

"It's a good idea," Chema replied.

"You two go along, I'll go home and give Mama the good news." Sabas said. "I'll see you tomorrow."

Cheno and Chema hugged Sabas and walked through the muddy streets to King and Kenedy's saloon and dancing hall in Levee Street. When they arrived there, the two story building was packed, a strong odor of alcohol, urine, tobacco and manure wafted from the entrance. Several girls served the tables. A few couples were dancing a polka played by an old piano and two fiddlers. Other couples were coming down or going up the stairs. Cheno and Chema knew about the available rooms upstairs for couples in need of privacy.

Once inside, they were greeted in a friendly way by the majority of those present. They found seats and through the cigar smoke, in the dim light of the kerosene lamps, Cheno noticed that the poker tables were busy. One of them was occupied by Steve Morris, his friend Andres Garza, two other Mexicans and two gringos unknown to him. At another table Cheno noticed that two of the Cubans with whom they had just made the deal were playing with one of the professional gamblers and a Mexican, he didn't recognize.

"The Cubans are playing with one of those thieves," Cheno said to Chema "I'm afraid he is going to take all of their money before they are able to pay for the cattle we are going to deliver."

"Yes, I see that," Chema answered, "but what can we do?"

"I'm going to join them," Cheno said.

"Be careful. Don't forget the gunslingers backing the gamblers," Chema warned.

"I'll take care. Watch my back," Cheno replied as he got up and walked toward the gambling table.

"May I join the party?" Cheno asked, addressing the Cubans who smiled and moved to make room for Cheno. The gambler just grimaced.

Cheno pulled out a chair, sat, lit a cigar and stared at the gambler.

"Opening bet is ten dollars. There is no upper limit," the gambler said. "Agreed?"

After everyone nodded in agreement, he said to Cheno. "My name is Fisher, by the way,"

"Juan Rodriguez is my name," the Mexican said, smiling at Cheno. "I'm from Monterrey, here in business."

"Glad to meet you," Cheno replied.

"Let's play," Fisher said as he dealt the cards, giving five to each player.

For the first two games the bets were small. They were won by one of the Cubans, the third went to Rodriguez. The fourth went to

Cheno. On the fifth game the Cubans became aggressive in their betting and it was won by Fisher.

"These cards are getting sticky. Let's get a new deck," Cheno said as he signaled a waiter for a new deck.

"What is wrong with these cards?" Fisher asked, grimacing, a menacing look in his eyes.

"As I said these cards are bent," Cheno answered, biting his cigar. His green eyes flashed as he stared to Fisher.

Two gunslingers, sensing trouble, started to walk toward the table. Chema, who also noticed the trouble, stood up and walked toward the table. A group of Mexicans seemed to become aware that something was wrong when the gunslingers moved in and also stood up.

"If it makes you comfortable, let's get a new deck," Fisher said, waiving the gunslingers back.

Jose Maria signaled the Mexicans to sit as he approached the table.

"If it is agreeable with you all," Cheno said without moving his eyes from Fisher "we'll have a dealer who isn't involved in the game." He pointed toward Chema. "You know my brother. Would you trust him?"

Rodriguez and the Cubans nodded in agreement. Fisher made a fist, clenched his jaws but also nodded.

"You are cheating," Cheno heard Garza screaming at the other table.

"That is a lie, and you will pay for it," somebody replied. Two gunshots shattered the air.

When Cheno turned around, he saw his friend Andres lying on the floor, a gun in his right hand. Morris and one of the gunslingers still held their guns, smoke coming out of them.

"He called me a cheater," Morris said, "He pulled his gun first." Cheno and Chema went to their friend, who tried to say something to Cheno, but gasped and died before he could say anything. .

Chema was about to jump toward Morris, but Cheno held him up.

"You, assassins," Chema screamed.

"He was a liar, and he pulled his gun first," Morris snapped.

Marshal Shears and Sheriff Brown came in. They heard the witnesses. All seemed to be in agreement. Garza had called Morris a cheater and had pulled his gun.

"It's clear that it was self defense," Marsahal Shears said.

"Are you letting these assassins free?" Cheno said angrily.

"You heard the witnesses. He pulled his gun first," Shears answered.

"But, they killed a man. At least they should stand trial," Chema screamed.

"It was self defense," Shears replied sounding indifferent.

Cheno stared at Brown, who shunned Cheno's eyes.

Several days later, a group of young girls, friends of Rafaela, were visiting at her home, in Matamoros. "Andale Rafaela, it might be interesting to know what the cards predict for your marriage." Micaela, one of the young girls said in Spanish.

"Tomasa is accurate, she read the cards for Refugio," Juanita intervened. "She told her that she would have profound sadness, but that later, she would find true happiness. One week after, Juventino, who was engaged to Refugio, fell from his horse and died. One year later Refugio married Tiburcio, who, as we all know, is very rich and now they live happily in Reynosa."

"I'm not sure," Rafaela said. "You know that I don't believe in witchcraft. Besides I'm afraid. If Cheno finds out that I went to that place he might get upset. He doesn't like that kind of thing."

"And who is going to tell him?" Griselda asked. "Come on, Rafaela. Let's do it just for the fun of it." They all giggled, pressing Rafaela.

"I'll go, but just for fun. I don't believe in it. But not a word about it to anybody, even your parents."

"Let's go now," Micaela said. "Before the night falls. Tomasa lives out of town and is not safe to be there at night."

Tomasa's humble shack was in the outskirts of Matamoros, it was made of wood sticks, with palm tree leaves for a roof. It was close to a beautiful branch of the river, home to dozens of ducks, peacocks, herons and many other birds. Besides witchcraft Tomasa was one of the town's midwives. The shack's walls and earthen floor were stained with old blood. Rafaela felt nauseated as she crossed from the door. But she felt calmer when she saw Tomasa, who was a short, robust woman in her late thirties, with fair skin. She was clean and the shack was neatly arranged. Rafaela felt intrigued by Tomasa's pleasant, flowery smell.

"How can I help you?" Tomasa asked the girls. She sat behind a wood table, a kerosene lamp; several decks of cards and a bowl filled with sand were on its top. Behind the table, Rafaela noticed two clean beds and in between them, a cage with two singing canaries and another held a green and blue parrot. "How can I help you?" the parrot repeated.

"She is getting married soon," Micaela said pointing to Rafaela. "She would like to know, what the cards say about her future."

Tomasa's yellow-green eyes stared at Rafaela who felt a cold chill run down her body.

"Well, little girl, I must warn you. The cards tell the truth. Some people don't like it. Do you want to hear all that cards say? Or do you prefer to hear only the pretty things?" Tomasa said smiling, as she played with the cards. Rafaela noticed that she had several teeth missing. She felt bothered as the parrot repeated Tomasa's last words. "... only the pretty things."

"I'm not afraid of the truth," Rafaela answered.

57

"As you wish," Tomasa said picking a deck of Mexican cards from the table. Her hands were small, soft, and chubby. "Pick a card," she ordered Rafaela, who obeyed pulling a card.

"El gallo," Tomasa said loudly, "your fiancée will make a good husband. Do you know what I mean?" she asked smiling, her eyes sparkling.

"Yes, of course," Rafaela answered, feeling embarrassed. The girls giggled and clapped happily.

"Pick another card," Tomasa said as she presented the deck to Rafaela.

Rafaela lifted her hand. "Maybe this is not a good idea," she said, feeling increasingly anxious.

"What is it.? Are you afraid of the truth?" Tomasa said firmly, holding the card deck in front of Rafaela, who felt pierced by Tomasa's feline eyes. A cold sweat ran down her back. Rafaela pulled a card.

"El caballo," Tomasa said loudly. This means wealth and power.

"Oh yes," Micaela said. "Cheno is indeed wealthy." The rest of the girls kept on giggling.

"Another," Tomasa said to Rafaela, who obeyed, feeling now as though she was in a kind of trance.

"El valiente, that means fighting and turmoil. Your man might be involved in something dangerous soon. But, if the card is right, he is courageous and valiant." Tomasa said. "Pick another."

Rafaela obeyed, showing the card to Tomasa, this time the woman paled and closed her eyes as soon as she saw the card. Rafaela felt again the cold chill running down her spine, the girls stopped giggling.

"La muerte," Tomasa whispered. "It means not only danger, but that people, dear to you, or your fiancée, will be involved with death after your marriage."

Rafaela paled. The girls looked at each other.

"I don't want hear anymore," Rafaela said turning around and running out, tears flowing down her cheeks.

The girls turned to follow her. Tomasa held Micaela. "You owe me two pesos," she said. Micaela looked into her silk purse, paid Tomasa and ran after Rafaela.

That same night a group of businessmen met at Stillman's home. "I have asked Charles to call you because there are new developments of which everyone should be aware," William Neale said. "Since the killing of Andres Garza, there has been turmoil among the Mexicans." He paused to sip from his whiskey. "Also, there are complaints about Marshal Shears and how he allows Sandoval to use his cruel methods of interrogation."

"They are a degenerate and inferior race. Shears methods are necessary for them to understand," Reverend Chamberlein intervened. "We have the burden to maintain peace and order. Cassos is the avenger sent by God to punish them for their sins. It is only natural that he is from their own race."

Charles Stillman felt a little nauseated and ashamed. I'm surrounded by idiots, he thought.

"There are rumors of revenge," Neale continued, "and the name of Cheno Cortina is frequently mentioned as their leader. He is becoming the strong man in town. Perhaps we should do something."

"Like what?" Francisco Iturria asked.

"Like continue spreading the rumor of his rustling cattle," Richard King intervened.

"I don't like that" Jose San Roman intervened. "Everybody knows that Cheno has no need to steal."

"But some of us here do," Charles Stillman intervened, a grin on his face. "Cortina might be a burden for our business, but for the time being he seems to be under control." He smoked his cigar looking around the room at the men present. "The seed of cattle rustling has fallen in good soil. Already businessmen in Matamoros are also afraid of him." The grin left his face. "We must admit that he is the natural leader of this people, he is gaining considerable political influence. If allowed he'll become the most important political figure in the Valley."

"I insist, they are an inferior race. We have the moral obligation of preventing a greaser ever getting to a position of power. That would stop progress." Hiram Chamberlein intervened. Iturria and San Roman looked at each other, upset.

Stillman's blue eyes pierced Chamberlein. He felt a bit ashamed, for years Mexicans had been his business partners. He appreciated how a simple shake of hands was enough to close a deal with them.

"Cortina and I have a business to settle," The harsh voice of Glaevecke brought Stillman back. "I'll be sure that the rumors of cattle rustling continue spreading." Glaevecke added.

"Even Sabas, his brother, is bothered by Cheno's continuous interferences in other people's business," Mifflin Kenedy said

"Cheno is getting married soon. That will mellow him." Iturria said smiling.

"Probably, but it will be better if you and Jose talk to Sabas," Stillman said dryly.

"For the time being there is a more important issue," Major Chapman said nervously, playing with his glass of whiskey. Everyone turned to look at him. "We have received orders to leave. Headquarters doesn't believe it's necessary to keep the Army in the area. Fort Brown will close in two weeks."

"What?" Neale shrieked. "That will leave us at the mercy of the Mexicans and Indians."

"At the mercy of Cortina and his followers," Glaevecke said.

"Under the circumstances that wouldn't be too bad after all," Stillman said rubbing his chin.

CHAPTER 9

Before the roosters welcomed the sunrise, Cheno and his vaqueros drove two hundred longhorns to the port of Bagdad located on the south side of the mouth of the Rio Bravo. The stars and the full moon provided enough light for them. Whistling, yelling, singing, they guided the herd. Knowing the river since they were children, they had no trouble finding where the river was shallow and in the dark they crossed, arriving to Bagdad before sunrise. Almost immediately, they were joined by Chema and his herd of two hundred. Tomas also arrived, leading the team of vaqueros that drove the four hundred longhorns sent by Sabas.

Although early, Bagdad was bustling. Dozens of boats, coming from every corner of the world, discharged their cargo. King and Kenedy steamboats bound to Roma, Texas, were loaded with goods destined to Monterrey, Zacatecas and Mexico City. Other smugglers also loaded their trains, some would go south, and some would go north. Mexican and American custom agents collected fees; most of it would end in their own pockets.

Hundreds of sailors speaking in strange tongues walked the muddy streets. The pungent smell of human and animal waste was muffled by the gentle sea breeze. Shacks converted into brothels, bars, coffee shops, restaurants were all open and busy, loud music and singing coming form most of them. It was a wild place and Cheno enjoyed it all. Shortly after sunrise, the Cubans had finished counting the cattle and paid the promised sum of five pesos in gold for each cattle head.

"I'll stop at Catchel's for breakfast," Cheno told Chema and Tomas after they had paid the vaqueros, "would you like to join me?"

"No, thank you," Tomas answered, "Sabas wants me to brand some cattle and water the rest. If you want, we'll meet tonight to celebrate."

"I don't know about tonight," Cheno replied "Rafaela wants us to discuss details of the wedding."

Chema and Tomas laughed. "My dear brother, you are being tamed," Chema said.

"Maybe, but I'm enjoying it," Cheno replied, also laughing. "Well, take care of yourselves." He waived, turned his dun and galloped toward Brownsville.

It was a gorgeous summer morning. Ever since he'd been a child, Cheno had enjoyed getting up early and watching the dazzling combination of yellow, orange, purple and red of the sunrise. When the colors hit the land it seemed as if earth and heaven embraced and for an instant, were one. Sunrises had always given him a perception of the greatness of nature. He felt humbled, but also felt as though he had a purpose for his life. That morning, the bright colors of the morning, reminded him of Rafaela. He felt happy. Life was wonderful, and everything was coming according to his plans. His horse, sensing the high spirit of his master, seemed to dance.

"Hey, Cheno, you look like you found a gold mine," somebody yelled when he arrived at Brownsville.

"Better than that," Cheno yelled back happily. Indeed, the dust lifted by his dun seemed to be golden.

When Cheno arrived at the market square, it was full with activity. Women buying fresh eggs, milk, fruits and vegetables. Butchers cutting the meat that would become somebody's lunch later in the day. Catchel's place was also busy. The smell of fried eggs, hot sauce, refried beans, menudo and above all fresh coffee with cinnamon filled the air. Cheno sat at an outdoors table and enjoyed watching the market's action

"Cheno, it's nice to see you again., What are you having today?" Catchel asked, cleaning the table.

"The menudo smell is wonderful. I'll have a plate, give me flour tortillas, and a cup of your delicious house coffee," Cheno replied.

When the food arrived, Cheno was about to take a spoonful of the spicy soup when he heard somebody singing a corrido in a loud and out of tune voice. He turned around and smiled when he saw Antonio Urbina, who was one of the vaqueros at his mother's ranch. Urbina was drunk, stumbling as he walked. Waving a bottle of tequila in his right hand, he sang, yelled, laughed, and bitched loudly. People let him pass by, smiling, Most of them knew that, though noisy, he was harmless.

"Hold it right there!" a harsh voice called out.

Cheno turned and frowned when he saw Marshall Shears walking toward Urbina, who stared at Shears.

"I don't want any trouble," Urbina said, "I'm just having a little fun. Would you like some tequila?" he added showing his rotten teeth and extending his arm, offering he bottle to Shears.

With a quick movement Shears pulled the bottle out of Urbina's hand smashing it on the ground, the sharp, almost musical sound of broken glass sounded like a sarcastic laugh to Cheno's ears.

"Amigo, why did you do that? That is good tequila" Urbina said as he was trying to stand still.

"Troublesome drunks aren't tolerated in this town," Shears said. "You are going to jail, and it will be better if you come peacefully."

"I'm not causing any trouble," Urbina said, angrily, "and I'm not going to jail."

He threw a right hand punch at Shears, who easily averted Urbina's fist. But the movement made Urbina loose his already precarious balance and he fell. Before he could get up, Shears kicked him in the belly, and then grabbed him around the neck, forcing him to stand up. Urbina resisted. Using his free hand Shears pulled his gun out of its holster, hitting Urbina in the face repeatedly.

Urbina's face became purple, saliva, blood and a couple of teeth streamed from his mouth.

"Darn dirty people, you don't seem to understand, but I'll teach you all a lesson you won't forget," Shears snarled as he kept on pistol whipping Urbina's face. The sharp sound of cracking bones filled the silence.

"Oh, God," a woman cried, covering her face.

"Please, somebody help him," another woman whispered.

Cheno got up, walking toward them, jaws tight, muscles tense, his red hair and beard looked like flames as the morning sea breeze and the bright sun hit him straight in the face. The rhythmic, high pitched musical sound of his Mexican spurs as he walked drew everyone's attention.

"Let him go," Cheno said, dryly. "He is a peaceful man, a bit rough when he gets drunk, but an honest, hard working, family man. Let me take him home." Cheno stopped, extending his right hand to free Urbina from the tight grip of Shears arm.

"What's up with you, darn greaser?" Shears replied, pulling away. "This one is going to jail, get out of the way."

"Please, this man is already hurt," Cheno said, slowly, his voice sounding harsh, and metallic to his own ears. He felt as if the veins of his arms might explode as he glared at Shears'.

"This greaser is hurt, eh?" Shears said a grin in his face, hitting Urbina's face again, whose nose poured a gush of blood.

With a quick movement, almost imperceptible to those present, Cheno pulled his gun. A sharp, whistle like, sound was heard, and Shears slumped, bleeding form his right shoulder. Cheno put the gun back in its holster and whistled for his obedient dun. Palomo pulled away from the hitching post and galloped toward Cheno, who, almost simultaneously, swung Urbina to the horse, mounted and dashed away.

Most of those present cheered and clapped. "Viva Cheno Cortinas!" someone yelled.

"Viva!' the crowd yelled back.

Cheno rode to "El Carmen," his mother's ranch. Once in there, he took Urbina to his shack.

"Take good care of him," he said to Teresa and Ramona, Urbina's wife and elder daughter, respectively. He then walked to the main house where he found his mother, sisters and Sabas. They had come out of the house, concerned, seeing Urbina's condition.

"What happened?" Sabas asked once they were inside.

63

Cheno grabbed a chair and sat. "I'll explain everything," he said, "but, first let me have a cup of coffee."

"You are a fool," Sabas said angrily, after Cheno had explained. "That quick temper of yours has always caused trouble. Shooting a US Marshal is a serious offense."

"What did you want me to do?" Cheno replied. "Stand in there and watch him hurt a good and honest man, pretending that nothing bad is happening?" He stared at Sabas. "What would you have done?"

"Nothing, Antonio is a drunk and a grown up man. He can take care of himself," Sabas replied, holding Cheno's stare. "I care only about my business." He looked to his sisters and mother, "and everyone should do the same." He looked back to Cheno. "These are difficult times, we should be thankful to the Americans, for letting us prosper along with them. You well know that our business is thriving."

"Prosperity," Cheno said, feeling frustrated and disgusted, "is that all you care about? Prosperity, business and money. According to you, as long as we do well, everyone else might as well go to hell. It is none of our business," Cheno raised his voice, clenched his fist, opening it he pointed to Sabas "Well, I got news for you, there is much more than that. There is dignity, honor, and respect. We are been treated as inferior when we are as good as anyone," He closed his fist again. "We are being treated as street dogs and according to you," he pointed to Sabas once more, "we should be happy to chew the bones thrown to us,"

"We have respect and we are honorable people. We harvest the fruit of our hard work, we care for ourselves, without asking for anyone else to come and help us. The others should take care of themselves," Sabas shouted, his face turning red, the muscles of his neck, tense.

"Oh, yes we are landowners, we have cattle and money and with it comes what you call respect. But, remember, that's a God's given blessing, it doesn't come free. We have to take care of those who are less fortunate." He stood up, paced the floor. The sound of his spurs projecting his contained anger.

"Please, Sabas, Cheno, calm yourselves," Carmen, their sister, said.

"You are both right," Estefana intervened, "God gave us the land, and with it, comes the duty to take care and protect those who are not as fortunate as we are," she said looking at Sabas. "But our first responsibility is toward ourselves, and in that Sabas is right. These are difficult times for us," she continued, turning to face Cheno. "We must find a way to make these duties compatible," she opened her arms as if embracing both of them, softening her voice.

At that moment, the door opened suddenly and Tomas entered, walking toward Cheno and embracing him.

"Word is spreading all over the Valley," he said, the creases on his face softening as he showed a broad smile. "It's great, it's just great. You have restored our dignity, our sense of pride. You have taught them a lesson," he said as he kept on shaking Cheno's shoulders. "The people are behind you. We are ready, just give us the signal and we'll start a rebellion to teach them that we are not puppets that can be pushed around."

Cheno passed his arm around Tomas' shoulders, smiling at him, but it was not his usual bright smile, the smile that gave his face a radiant look. This time it was a dull, sad smile.

"Thank you, Tomas," he said. "It's nice to know it. But I don't think that we'll need to start a rebellion. This time Sabas is right," he added pointing to his brother.

Cheno was going to say something else, when the door opened again. This time Chema came through it, his steps sounding sharp as his boots hit in the wooden floor as he walked toward Cheno, hugging him.

"I came as soon as I heard the news. I'm happy to see that you are well. What are we going to do now?" he asked Cheno as he pulled a chair and sat.

"We are going to do nothing," Cheno answered. "I'm going to give myself up and offer an apology to Shears."

"That is the right thing to do," Sabas said smiling, as he stood up and clapped Cheno on the shoulder

"I'm not so sure about that," Chema said, looking pensive and surprised by his brother's answer.

"If they dare to touch you, there will be a riot," Tomas said angrily.

"Don't get me wrong," Cheno said, "I'm not giving up my beliefs, I will keep on fighting for our rights. But we'll do it the peaceful way first. We'll fight through the legal and political arena."

"That's the way many of our friends and neighbors have been forced to sell for peanuts, or worse, abandon their grants," Chema said.

"We'll keep on fighting for them and for ourselves, but as I said, the right way. We have chosen to become Americans, so we'll accept their law," Cheno replied, getting his hat and turning to leave. As soon as he walked out of the door, he stopped a surprised look on his face. Outside there was a large number of mounted vaqueros that as soon as Cheno walked out, they let out a triumphant cheer.

"I told you, we are ready," Tomas said laughing and slapping Cheno in the back.

Cheno smiled. "Thank you." he said, in a loud voice, so that everyone would hear him, "but this is something I must do alone."

"We'll ride with you," Tomas said. "That way, we'll be sure that they won't harm you."

Cheno mounted, turned his dun facing the vaqueros. "Listen," he shouted, "we are going to Brownsville in peace. Once there we'll ask for justice, but no one should be hurt, no even a hen or a street dog."

"Viva Cheno Cortina!" Tomas yelled.

"Viva!" the vaqueros yelled back. A cantata of acute, savage, almost musical bellows followed.

Meanwhile, in Brownsville, a group of prominent citizens had gathered at Mayor Power's office on the second floor of Market Building. Among them, Charles Stillman, Francsisco Iturria, Richard King, Reverend Hiram Chamberlein, Jose San Roman, Sheriff Brown, William Neale and Adolphus Glaevecke. Stillman looked at the long, worried, tense, facial expressions. They shook hands nervously. Stillman noticed that some of the hands were sweaty and some seemed to be trembling. Only King, Iturria and San roman seemed to be calm and relaxed.

"The town is in turmoil, "Reverend Chamberlein said, as he wiped the sweat from his forehead and hands, his blue eyes cold and unsympathetic. "The Mexicans seem to be ready for a riot, nothing good can come if a US Marshall is shot without punishment," he added.

"Judge Watrous has already extended an order for indictment against Cortina," Sheriff Brown said, "but the Judge has stated that, in his opinion, the indictment should be for Marshal Shears. The judge doesn't approve his methods." He hesitated for a moment before continuing. "One must admit that Marshal Shears methods are brutal, but even worse are the methods he allows Sandoval, his assistant, in the treatment of prisoners. Cassoos is particularly cruel when the prisoner is an Indian or a Mexican."

"They are an inferior and brutal race," Reverend Chamberlein said, "firmness is required to make them understand law and order."

"Although, I Agree that firmness is required, there is no need for cruel methods," King intervened, looking at Reverend Chamberlein, "these people work hard, they are humble, obedient and loyal if one knows how to treat them."

"I agree with you, but on the other hand, with all the newcomers, most of them just passing through, on their way to California, with all the brothels, bars and cantinas that have opened; we need the semblance of law and order. Marshall Shears provides that, so we can keep on with our business." Samuel Belden said a touch of nervousness in his voice.

"But justice should be equal for all," Jose San Roman insisted.

"We all agree on that," Belden replied.

"We are not here to judge Marsahll Shears methods," Glaevecke intervened, "but to decide what is going to be done about Cortina. He does as he pleases. He just got away with the indictment of cattle rustler and now, this."

Stillman could not prevent a surprised and sarcastic grin coming to his face. Although Glaevecke had been useful to him, and to most of those present, every time the business at hand was not an honest one, he barely could tolerate Glaevecke.

"The indictment to arrest Cortinas is there," Sheriff Brown said, "but, who is going to arrest Cheno?" He shook his head. "I would prefer to resign from my post before taking him into custody. I happen to believe that Cortina's did the right thing. I've never approved of Shears methods."

"Shears has powerful friends in Austin, and as Samuel said he provides us with some sense of law and order. Even you have to obey him." Stillman said, looking at Brown. "So he will continue in his post. On the other hand, if Cortina is arrested, we'll face not a riot but a rebellion, and we are not ready for that." He paused to think for a moment. "I suggest we let the indictment rest. I'm sure Sabas will control his little brother."

"Under the circumstances, that is a sensible advice," Iturria agreed.

"Are there other suggestions?" Mayor Powers asked, pausing for a moment to look at all the present. "Does anyone oppose Mr. Stillman's suggestion?" he asked after no one had said a word. "Well, then, it is agreed that, for the time being, no attempt to arrest Cheno Cortina will be made. I suggest that some of us talk to Marshall Shears regarding his methods. Thank you for your assistance. Have a good day, gentlemen."

The late afternoon sun was blazing, the town barely coming out of siesta, when the rhythmic, drum like, sound of a troop of horses hooves aroused its inhabitants.

"Cheno is coming, Cheno is coming," barefoot children running at full speed, yelled. Men, women, children, old and young, all came out to the street, cheering their hero, the man they considered their protector, the one who had showed courage and stood up for them.

Trotting his horse, Cheno rode straight, his reins in his left hand, he tugged his broad hat to his back, waving occasionally with his right hand. The vaqueros laughed, waving at their friends and screeching along with them. Nervous businessmen looked trough their windows, their employees hurriedly closing the front doors, their guns ready in case they were needed. Surrounded by a cloud of dust, the horde arrived at the Marshall's office on Elizabeth Street.

"Keep the peace," Cheno said to Tomas as he dismounted and walked toward the office.

"They know how to behave, "Tomas replied. "I'll go with you. "

Inside, Marshall Shears, with a sling made of a rough red cotton fabric, holding his right arm across his chest, was sitting in a rocking chair, his legs resting on a table that acted as a desk. Standing at his side was Jesus Sandoval, a machete hanging from his waist.

"What do you want?" Shears asked, his voice cold, an ominous shine in his blue eyes.

"We come in peace," Cheno said, standing in front of the desk,

67

holding Shears' look. Tomas moved to Cheno's side, keeping an eye on Sandoval.

"That doesn't look peaceful," Shears said, pointing to the crowd outside.

"As I said, we have come in peace," Cheno replied. "I'm here to tell you that I meant no harm to you, but you didn't give me another choice. I can see that no serious harm was done." Cheno pointed to Shears right arm.

Shears frowned, a menacing look in his eyes. "No harm done, eh?" he said, moving his legs from the desk and standing up. "You shoot me," he shouted, "son of a bitch, you shoot a United States Marshal, and you come here saying that no harm was done?" He took a couple of steps toward Cheno. Tomas went to his gun, Sandoval to the machete. Cheno held Shears' look, not moving at all.

"There is an indictment for your arrest, and you come here to tell me that no harm was done," Shears snarled.

Cheno waved that aside, determined to deliver his message. "I told you that I am here in peace, but also I want you to know that we won't tolerate any more abuse. All we want is fairness, no more whipping of harmless drunk Mexicans, Indians or even white people for that matter." He pointed once more to Shears right arm. "If necessary I'll pay for any expense you might have incurred in taking care of that."

Shears spat on the dusty, wooden floor. "You arrogant, damn greaser, you believe that just by coming here and offering to pay, and all will be forgotten. Keep your dirty money. I'll continue doing my job the way I see it fit. Today, I won't arrest you, but a fool like you sooner or latter will end up in jail. I'm looking forwards to that day."

"We'll leave the way we came. You have been warned. We won't tolerate anymore abuse." Cheno turned and walked toward the door. Tomas exchanged menacing looks with Sandoval before following Cheno.

That night Cheno visited Rafaela at her home in Matamoros.

"Cheno I'm so worried, Shears already hated you. Now I'm afraid he will do everything within his power to harm you." Rafaela said after Cheno had told her all the details of the incidents of the day. With a concerned look in her face, she reached out to touch Cheno's hand.

"Let's not worry about that. It will be better if we talk about the wedding." Cheno replied smiling and holding her hand.

CHAPTER 10

"Cheno, are you nervous?" Chema asked, laughing, as he stood up and walked toward Cheno giving him a friendly slap in the back. "Here, brother, let me help you with that bow in your tie."

"Little brother it's not everyday that one gets married, "Cheno replied, lifting his neck, allowing Chema to make the bow in his elegant, red silk, charro tie.

"Every time we go to the brothels in Bagdad, you are the favorite of the girls. They fight for a chance to get you. And now, you tell me you are nervous because you are getting married?" Chema kept on laughing.

"You damn well know that it's not the same. Rafaela is a virgin. Besides this is a lifetime commitment, not just for one fucking moment," Cheno snapped, feeling embarrassed, blood flowing to his cheeks.

"Well, well, my dear brother, don't get upset," Chema said smiling; "there you are, well dressed with a nice and beautiful bow in your tie."

"Let's go, I don't want to be late," Cheno said, smiling. Upset with himself for snapping at his brother.

They were at the family home in Matamoros, and as they walked out of the bedroom they met with Estefana, Carmen and other women, friends and members of the family, who were waiting for them in the living room. Cheno felt impressed when he saw them all elegantly dressed and adorned with expensive gold earrings and necklaces.

"Son, that dress really fits you well." Estefana said, proudly, walking towards Cheno and kissing him in the cheek, holding his hands. Carmen and the other women surrounded Cheno, all talking at the same time, sounding like chicken around a rooster. Cheno, more comfortable among cows, wild horses, rough vaqueros and Indians, felt increasingly nervous, embarrassed, bothered by the unwanted attention, nauseated by the strong odor of cologne.

"Well, ladies, thank you for your compliments. Rafaela and I are happy with your presence," Cheno said, trying to be polite. "But, now, it will be better if we leave. Father Nicolas must already be waiting at the Cathedral"

For the occasion Cheno wore a dark brown charro suit specially ordered for him by Estefana. It had been hand made with wool gabardine. To join the chest part of the jacket with the sleeves at the level of the underarm white silk was used to allow for freedom of movement.

The suit was completed by a red silk bow tie with white silk needle-work and a broad sombrero made of the same material as the suit. It was all enhanced by elegant silver embroidery on the side of the pant legs and all around the edge of the sombrero. The buttons of his jacket were made of solid silver, material that was also used to cover the tips of the dark brown, charro boots that covered only up to his ankles. His favorite horse, Palomo, the dun tamed by him, was saddled with a hand carved leather saddle, also decorated with silver figures at the tips of each leather covered stirrups.

Cheno mounted, Sabas, Tomas and Chema riding along with him, wore elegant charro suits. Their horses also had beautiful, hand carved leather saddles, together, they made an impressive platoon. As they walked their horses toward Hidalgo square, people in the street yelled congratulations to Cheno, as they passed by, wishing him years of happiness in his marriage. He responded by smiling and waiving.

Father Nicholas greeted them at the entrance of the Cathedral; he guided Cheno through the main corridor, asking him to stand in front of the altar to wait for his bride. Cheno felt his heart pounding, knees shaking, hands sweating, the smell of fresh flowers made him nauseated again, it was then that he became aware of the white figure coming through the main door, walking toward him.

He asked himself if he was dreaming and an angel was approach-ing, his heart pounded heavier as the heavenly figure got closer, he then recognized Rafaela, her dark eyes shining, a wave of her black hair covering her forehead glittered flashes of blue when hit by the light filtered by the stained glass windows. The white veil, framed her face, enhancing the natural color of her cheeks. Cheno made an effort to hold himself from jumping, hugging, kissing, and possessing her right there. Instead, he smiled, extended his hand to help her, barely notic-ing the brocade enhancing her dress, he guided her to the recliners, covered with white silk. They both kneeled in front of the altar.

The mass went fast, Cheno answered with a clear and loud, "Yes, I do!" when asked and felt exhilarated when he heard Rafaela also reply-ing "Yes, I do," the sound of her voice like celestial music to Cheno's ears. He felt so happy that he had to contain himself not to cry.

After mass, they walked the aisle, Rafaela's hand on Cheno's forearm, all the presents clapping cheerfully. Once outside, whistling fire crackers burst in the air, a calandria, a buggy decorated with fresh flowers, took the newlyweds back to Estefana's home. The wedding party was already on its way. The streets around the house had been washed the day before, to make them firm, so those wishing to dance could do so to the music of several musical groups, playing Mexican polkas and corridos. Barbacoa just out of the steaming pit, hot sauce and tortillas, also just out of the oven were served to everyone who pre-sented a plate. Tequila, mezcal, freshly squeezed lemonade, tamarindo,

Jamaica flower drinks, also were served. Children feasted on watermelon, pineapple slices along with prickled tunas. The important people were being served inside of the house. Cheno and Rafaela personally greeted all the guests. A couple of times they went to the street, to join the party there, mingling and dancing along the common people who showed their love and appreciation with hundreds of small presents. At dusk, Cheno and Rafaela were ready to retire to the bedroom already prepared for them.

Cheno walked straight to the bedroom, Rafaela went to an adjacent room to prepare and receive instructions from her mother and other women, a feminine ceremony with a long tradition.

Once in the bedroom, Cheno poured himself a shot of tequila, but put it aside immediately, not wanting to have an alcoholic breath. Slowly, carefully, he started undoing the bow tie, taking it off, and then taking of the entire suit. Once undressed, for the first time in his life, he got into a cotton sleeping gown that went all the way down to his ankles. He smiled. How people get into this every day? He asked himself. A soft knock in the door called his attention.

"Come in," he said, a tremor of nervousness in his voice.

The door opened, Rafaela, dressed in a long, white silk, night gown, entered. Her gown was beautiful, covering her entire body, but still allowing for her feminine curves to show through, her long black hair, hanging freely over her shoulders. Cheno, feeling exhilarated started walking toward her, extending his arms. He stopped suddenly on noticing a surprised smile in her face.

"What's wrong?" he asked, his voice trembling, with a touch of anxiety.

"Nothing, it is only that this the first time I see you in your sleeping clothes," Rafaela answered, her voice was soothing, and she smiled, extending her arms to get his.

"Well…" Cheno started saying, still a bit anxious.

"Ssh," she whispered, "you look handsome as always." Moving closer she kissed him on the cheek.

Regaining control of himself, Cheno hugged her gently, carefully ran his hand down her back, caressing her softly, cautious, like if she was made of porcelain that might suddenly break. Gently he guided her to the bed and she followed.

Tenderly, lovingly, Cheno kissed her. Soft, humid kisses, first on the forehead, then the cheeks, barely touching her lips, going down to kiss her neck and shoulders, while at the same time, carefully, always gently, undoing the lace of her night gown, helping her to pull her arms out, freeing with the movement her firm, virginal, breasts. Feeling her fingers caressing the back of his neck, he barely touched her nipples with his lips, her body shaking slightly, responding to his caresses. He took of his night gown; he went on kissing, caressing Rafaela, removing her gown.

Now, both of them fully naked, their bodies rubbing each other, the sweat pouring out of their bodies acting as lubricant, allowing them to use their bodies to caress each other. Cheno could now feel her whole body trembling in his arms, he kept on kissing, caressing her, alert to her responses, patient, as if he were taming a wild horse, waiting for her until she was ready to be taken. She responded to his caresses passionately, instinctively, arousing him even more.

Outside of the bedroom, Estefana, Cristina, Rafaela's mother, Carmen and other women, their ears glued to the bedroom door, listened carefully. The rhythmic, squeaking, muffled, sound coming from the bedroom made them smile, making an effort not to giggle they looked at each other, nodding their heads approvingly. Outside, the music, food, drinks and dancing continued for two days more.

A couple of weeks later, a group of prominent citizens gathered at Stillman's house drawing room. As customary at these reunions and Stillman being a first class host, they smoked Cuban cigars, drank French cognac served in crystal glasses and sat in comfortable leather chairs. The windows were left open to allow the evening sea breeze to mitigate the heat of the summer.

"Well, now that Cheno has married, we can assume that the wild puma is tamed and has become a pussycat," Glaevecke said laughing at his own joke.

"We can't be sure about that. Besides, Cheno's wildness has been handy for some of us here today, when we needed someone to blame for our mischief," Stillman replied, dryly. "But that's another matter. Today I have asked all of you, my friends and partners, to meet with me because there are important events approaching," he continued, frowning as he spoke. "My partners in Mexico City tell me that the country is now not only in a deep political struggle, as it has been since it's independence from Spain, but on top of that, it has become unable to pay it's debt to several European countries, mainly England, France and Spain. And these countries are threatening to invade Mexico to assure payment." He concluded, lighting a cigar.

"A firm and steady government in Mexico could be beneficial for all. Mexicans are a wild and uncivilized race, they need a firm hand to control them, they are not ready for Democracy as Americans are," Pastor Chamberlein intervened, "a monarchic style of government will be good for them," he paused, "I'll drink to that," he added, taking a sip of his cognac.

"Maybe so," Stillman said, "but this isn't the only news. There is more, that is at least as important. My business partners in New York and New Orleans have sent information that, along with the news from Mexico, could harm our business." He paused for a moment, pensive. "Or it might be an extraordinary opportunity if we are careful and know how to take advantage of the upcoming circumstances," he added, his business instinct feeling the exuberance of the challenge.

"What news are you talking about?" Iturria asked leaning forwards and looking a bit nervous.

Stillman continued smiling; enjoying the suspense he'd created. "There are strong rumors that the South might secede from the Union." He paused again, choosing his words carefully. "That is, if that clown from Illinois, Abraham Lincoln, is elected president."

"He is an abolitionist," Kenedy intervened. "The South won't tolerate any interference in its right to hold and maintain the slave system," he paused frowning, also pensive.

"Which side would Texas take?" San Roman asked, his voice slightly trembling.

"The South, of course," Reverend Chamberlein replied.

"If the South secedes, it could mean war," Richard King said as he absently scratched his head.

"That the South would easily win, have no doubt about that. A Southern gentleman is worth more than forty Yankees," Chamberlein boasted.

"But, how is all of this beneficial to us?" Iturria asked.

"We are in a privileged geographical position," Stillman answered, talking slowly, carefully choosing his words, measuring and weighing them in his mind before allowing them to come out of his mouth. "The Mexican government's high taxes on imported and exported goods, are an effort to control the flow of commerce. It has allowed only one port to serve as the entrance or exit of all goods and that is through the Port of Veracruz," he paused for a moment, running his blue eyes through each man in the room to be sure that they were listening. "Now," he continued, "If the European come and block Veracruz, Mexico will need alternative ports, Tampico and particularly, Bagdad will be the logical choices."

"I see," Iturria intervened, as if he was reading Stillman's mind. "If Bagdad is the chosen port, as in all probability it will be, with the monopoly of the steamboat in the Rio Grande established by our partners Kenedy and King, and our connections in Monterrey, Zacatecas, San Luis and Mexico City, we could control every aspect of business in Mexico." He smiled,

Stillman felt proud of his pupil and soul mate.

"That makes sense, but I still fail to see how a war between North and South would be beneficial to us," King said, his left hand now rubbing the beard on his chin.

"If there is war," Stillman replied, still careful with his choice of words, "the North having a better Navy, almost certainly will block every port in the South. So the Southern states will need a safe outlet for the backbone of their economy: Cotton. Your ranch Saint Gertrudis, in the middle of the Wild Horse Dessert, is in a perfect position to establish a route for trains to any part of the lower Rio Grande and once again, thanks to the steamboat system that you have established, we have a link to the Port of Bagdad. And since it is on the Mexican side of the border, can you see it? The European countries need the cotton from the South; even the Northern States need it. They all will come here to get it, and we are in position to control it all. The business to and from Mexico and the business from practically the entire United States," feeling almost overwhelmed by the grandeur of his project he smiled broadly as he rarely did, his blue eyes sparkling as he moved his left hand to take a puff from his cigar.

"That's brilliant," Kenedy said, also with a broad smile on his face.

"Indeed, it *is* brilliant," San Roman intervened, "but there is only one problem with that scheme." Stillman looked at him inquisitively.

"What's that?" Steven Powers asked.

"There is unrest among the population in town, especially among the Mexicans," San Roman replied, pausing for a moment before continuing. "As we are all well aware Marshall Shears methods are now tougher. It seems to me that he is a member of those parties trying to stir up a new war with Mexico."

"Are you talking about the Know Nothing Party?" Powers asked.

"Yes, indeed and the Order of the Lone Star of the West. These semi-secret societies are looking to create reasons to start another war with Mexico in order to grab more land, but at the same time they would love to get rid of the Mexicans," San Roman continued.

"Or at least make them civilized, that's the burden of the White men," Chamberlein intervened.

"Shears methods not only have become tougher since the incident with Cortina," Powers said, "but he also encourages Cassoos cruel methods of interrogation , specially when it comes to deals with Mexican peasants, vaqueros or Indians," he added.

"Perhaps, he is challenging Cheno," Sheriff Brown said, "he vowed to act if Shears continued with these tactics." He wiped the sweat from his forehead before taking a sip of cognac.

"Cheno is the only one who could organize a rebellion," Stillman said, then shrugged, "but, once again, there is good news, Tijerina has told me that there are plans to ask Cheno to join the Mexican Army and send him to central Mexico, as the government in Mexico is getting ready to repel the invasion." He thought for a moment. "In reality, Cheno is a dreamer, he is naïve and loves to fight for lost causes, and when he finds out about the imminent invasion, chances are good that he will accept."

"Sabas will keep him in check, and if he doesn't do it, Rafaela will tame him for sure," Glaevecke insisted.

"I wouldn't be sure about that," Stillman replied, "if we want to take advantage of the almost certain upcoming events in both countries, it will help us to plan how to maintain full control of the Valley."

"We should start by inviting Sabas to join these meetings," Iturria said.

"I would go along with that," Powers said. "He might help to convince Cheno to join the Mexican Army."

Everyone nodded in agreement.

"It will also help if there is fairness in the justice system," Iturria continued. "Mexicans have been murdered and the guilty are not only free, but not even an indictment for their arrest has been issued."

Stillman noticed how Neale's face flushed.

"Also, Mexicans ranchers should not be forced to sell or abandon their properties," San Roman added.

Kenedy and King looked at each other a sarcastic grin in their faces"

"More important would be to convince the Governor to reopen Fort Brown," Belden intervened for the first time.

"Under the present circumstances that would be difficult," King said. "It would better if we organize our own group of rangers."

"As you and Kenedy have already done," San Roman said.

"Those rangers could become handy someday," Iturria said.

"Indeed," Stillman said. "It is then agreed that Sabas will be invited to join us in future reunions, King and Kenedy will organize rangers that will help in keeping peace."

Those present nodded and grumbled their agreement.

"Great, now I would like to propose a toast," Stillman said, standing up and extending his right arm, holding a glass half filled with cognac.

"Everyone also stood up and extended their glasses. "A toast," they repeated in chorus.

"A toast to an adventurous and successful business, a toast to the future," Stillman said in a loud voice, drinking all the fluid from his glass.

"To business and the future," they repeated in chorus, also emptying their glasses.

CHAPTER 11

It was a dark night. The purple and black clouds looked ominous, a storm was brewing, but at the moment, only occasional, small drops of rain dampened at King's broad-brimmed hat. He was a few miles away from his ranch, mounted on his pinto horse, watching how in the distance, red, yellow, orange and blue blazes illuminated the darkness. The brightness of the distant flames made him smile.

That will be a lesson for all those who dare to resist progress, he thought. Mexicans are humble, obedient, loyal and hard workers, I'll give them that, but most of them are like children; they don't know how to make the most of their land. They feel happy and satisfied if they can raise enough crops to feed their families. Damn fools, they should have accepted my offer. I'm a generous man, and I'll maintain the offer, even now that those properties have become almost worthless.

Tomorrow, Powers will talk to those who chose to stay and repeat the offer. It all will be legal. He shook his head. That fool of Cortina did us a favor in helping Powers become Brownsville's Mayor, Stephen has always been a good and shrewd lawyer but now he has become an expert in the legal nuisances of real state along the border. The sound of horse's hooves galloping toward him, called his attention.

"What's the matter, boys?" King asked, as the riders approached, he was feeling cheerful, "has a volcano broken loose?" he asked as his pinto danced.

"They got a dose they'll never forget. Five Mexican ranches just caught fire," Capt. Hines Clark, replied, as he, along with twenty- five mounted men got close. "Everything is burning, but the hide houses," he added.

"Mmpgh," King grumbled, "Well, there are plenty of teams and wagons at Gertrudis Ranch. Go get the hides, sell them and put the money in your pockets."

"We wouldn't like to fool with hides when we can't prove how we got them," Hines replied.

"Then go back and burn them," King snapped. "Don't leave them for the Mexicans." A thunderous lightning brightened the darkness as heavy rain drops started to fall. .

A few days later, Adolphus Glaevecke, Tomas Vazquez, Jean Vela and other vaqueros were busy branding cows at the edge of the desert of the wild horse. Although they were close to the beach and half way between Brownsville and Santa Gertrudis Ranch, the place was so dry and hot that the local vaqueros knew that particular spot as "el desierto de la muerte,"- the dessert of the dead-, and tried to avoid it. At that particular moment, the soothing sound of the sea waves caressing the beach and the deep green, purple, blue colors of the Laguna Madre made the scene almost pleasant, but the heat and the menacing appearance of some of the vaqueros would have prevented anyone from attempting to get close.

Some of the cowboys were busy corralling the longhorns; others helped Jean and Tomas in the branding. They all were in a good mood.

"Hey, Jean be sure that Garza's brand is visible when you apply Cortina's on top of it," Glaevecke yelled to Vela. "Your stepfather might get upset if we don't get this job right."

"Captain Kenedy is not as tough as my boss Captain King," Vazquez intervened, "but Adolphus is right, we must leave enough evidence to get that cabron of Cortina out of the way." He grinned, "Cheno is going to have a nice surprise when Garza's stolen cattle are found at his ranch. This time there will be the confession from some of his loyal vaqueros."

"How is that?" Vela asked.

"Marshal Shears has already been made aware of the stolen cattle," Vazquez replied, a cynical smirk on his face, "even before it was stolen, and he has already sent Sandoval to find and capture some of Cortina's vaqueros. You know, with Jesus' methods everyone sings like a canary," All the present laughed.

"We've branded forty longhorns," one of the vaqueros said. "Do you want us to continue, or what do you want us to do with the rest of the cattle?" he asked as he went for a jar of fresh water.

"No, that's enough. Let's kill the rest and get the hides, we'll sell them in Bagdad" Glaevecke answered as he looked up. "Let's give the vultures a feast." He let out a guttural, cruel laugh.

"Cheno, you have built a nice house here. Allow me to congratulate you and Rafaela once again," Antonio Tijerina said as he sat in the bejuco chair offered by Cheno. They were in the living room in the newly built house in the San Jose Ranch. "We all had a good time at your wedding. People are still talking about it." Tijerina continued, smiling.

"Thanks," Cheno replied, pulling up a chair, "would you like a cup of coffee?" Pointing to Rafaela, who was approaching with a tray.

"Thanks, Rafaela," Tijerina said as he accepted a steaming cup of coffee. He took a sip before continuing. "Cheno, our motherland is in deep trouble and she will require the help of all of her children."

"Yes, I know," Cheno answered, holding his cup of coffee with his right hand, pensive. "But, I'm an American now and I'd like to settle down and prosper as such."

"Ja, Cheno, don't fool yourself," Tijerina replied. "Do you really believe that the Gringos will let you be one of them? To achieve your political ambitions? To get to a position of real power and influence?"

"Well, Sabas, Iturria, San Roman, among others, are successful. My ranch is also doing well and along with my brothers I'm a prosperous rancher," Cheno replied. "Besides, my influence was instrumental in the election of Brown as Sheriff and Steven Powers as Mayor." He smiled, suddenly feeling nervous, his words sounding hollow to himself. He knew what Tijerina was about to say.

"Hah!" Tijerina snapped a grin on his face. "Your brother Sabas, like Iturria and San Roman are doing well because they don't interfere, and as a matter of fact, participate in their business, legal or not." He stared at Cheno. "And the election of Sheriff Brown and Mayor Powers, how has it helped you? Have they gotten you out of trouble? Have they stopped the abuse against vaqueros, peons, Mexicans in general, and everyone who is not as wealthy as yourself or them?"

"Well," Cheno started to say, "I don't know." He felt a sudden itch in his right cheek, and shifted anxiously in his chair as he scratched with his right hand.

"Come and join the Mexican Army," Tijerina continued before Cheno could say anything more. "You have the legal rights to your property. You could come back whenever you want. You know that your brother Chema and perhaps, even Sabas, will help you in that matter."

"I don't know, I am the one to whom people look for help whenever they are in trouble" Cheno said hesitantly.

"Yes, that's true, on both sides of the river," Tijerina said. "You are a natural born leader, you care about people, you look out not only for yourself, but for the good of all regardless of their social status. We all know that, and that's the reason I'm asking you to join the Mexican Army."

"And what about Rafaela?" Cheno asked, pensive, still rubbing his right cheek. "We just got married."

"I'll support and respect your decision, whatever it might be," Rafaela said, entering the room.

"You were listening," Cheno smiled, getting up and extending his arms toward her. Tijerina stood up as soon as he noticed Rafaela enter the room.

"Yes, I'm sorry but I couldn't help it," Rafaela apologized. "I sensed that the conversation had something to do with both of us." She fell into Cheno's arms and they embraced each other, tenderly.

"I'm glad you did," Cheno said after they were seated. "Because this is a matter in which I'll need your advice."

"As I said," Rafaela replied, "I'll support you." She turned and looked at Tijerina. "How certain are you about the foreign invasion to Mexico?"

"It's a fact." Tijerina answered. "Mexico is going to need the help of all of its children."

The sound of a galloping horse, approaching at full speed called their attention. They got up and walked toward the door. The rapid, rhythmic sound of the horse's hooves gave Cheno a sense of desperation, a premonition of disaster. A chill ran up his back.

Shortly afterwards Tomas Cabrera burst into the room, sweating profusely, his shirt and cotton pants soaked through. Beneath the perspiration on his face Cheno noticed an expression of furious anxiety. Tomas stood in front of them for a moment, making an effort to catch his breath. Cheno feared the worst as he watched his friend trying to calm his heavy breathing. The wrinkles on his face looked deeper. Tomas raised his arms, looking up, as if he was asking heaven for help, opening and closing his fists in a furious sequence, he grimaced and moved his mouth as if having difficulty finding where to start.

"They are dead, killed," he finally said, "dismembered by that assassin at the service of Shears," he added.

"Who is dead?" Cheno asked, "What are you talking about?" Cheno felt the muscles in the back of his neck getting tense.

"Teofilo and Lencho were arrested yesterday by Jesus Sandoval on orders from Marshall Shears. They were accused of rustling cattle for you," Tomas voice was loud, and he waived his hands as he spoke, visibly upset. "Jesus tied them to the horses, time after time, until they said what he wanted to hear," Tomas paused, closing his eyes, tightening his jaws, taking a deep breath before continuing, "After they'd confessed, Jesus let the horses rip their heads from their bodies." His eyes sparkled, furious. Cheno noticed that they were red and wet. "That cabron!" Tomas added clenching his fists.

Cheno muscles tightened, his heart beating fast in his chest, the blood pounding in his head.

Rafaela was sobbing loudly.

Tijerina had his fists clinched shaking his head.

"An indictment against you has been issued," Tomas continued, "Shears is getting men to come and arrest you."

Hearing it, Rafaela stopped sobbing, and grasped Cheno's arm firmly. "Cheno," she said, "you are joining the Mexican Army, today."

Cheno looked at Rafaela, surprised. He frowned, looking alternatively at Tomas and Tijerina.

"Get the horses. We are leaving for Matamoros; I will join the Mexican Army," Cheno said to Tomas, then turned, hugged Rafaela and kissed her, tenderly, gently. Suddenly he was feeling surprisingly calm.

September 21, 1859, Matamoros, Mexico. Cheno, Tomas, Antonio, Chema and the rest of the men were celebrating the commemoration of the consummation of Mexico's independence. They were at their garrison in Fortin Bravo, just north of Matamoros. Several bottles of tequila and mezcal had been opened and emptied. They were in a cheerful and patriotic mood. The traditional "vivas" and "hurras" to Mexican independence had already been yelled.

"Hey, men what about all those who have killed Mexicans and gone unpunished?" Ceferino Cabrales suddenly yelled, his face flushed by too much tequila.

"Yeah, what about Marshal Shears who mistreats Mexicans just because they are such?" someone else shouted.

"What about George Morris?" Another man yelled, throwing his glass against the wall in anger. "He cheats and kills anyone who dares to protest."

"Don't forget Billy Neale" A voice chimed in. "He killed two of our friends, just because a woman preferred them to him."

"Yes. What about them?" Tomas asked Cheno. "Also, what about Adolfo, your cousin? What about Jesus Sandoval? Are they going to stay unpunished?" Tomas stared at Cheno waiting for an answer.

"No," Cheno replied, "their misdeeds won't go unpunished."

CHAPTER 12

Sept 28 1859. Three o'clock in the morning. Toads and crickets serenaded the moon. A coyote feasted on a wild duck caught at one of the resacas. Relieved by the gentle fall weather from the summer heat, the roosters and all of Brownsville were sleeping soundly when the trembling sound of galloping horses, wild yells, gunshots and men screaming interrupted the night's peace.

"Viva Cheno."

"Viva Cortina."

"Viva México! Death to the gringos! Free the Mexicans!" the shouts rang out, waking everyone.

Cheno and seventy five of his men galloped into Brownsville through Elizabeth Street. They rode all the way until they reached the abandoned Fort Brown. Once in there, Tomas took a Mexican flag from his saddlebags and was about to raise it up the flag pole, when Cheno held his arm.

"Whether we like it or not, this is now United States soil. The Mexican flag won't look right in there," Cheno said, in a gentle but firm tone of voice, as he took the flag from Tomas' hands. He turned to face the men.

"Boys, we are here to bring justice to those who have mocked it, until now," he told them. "Also, all of those who have been imprisoned for no fault of their own will be set free. But, no harm should be done to innocent people. Whoever of you disobeys these orders will be severely punished. Am I clear?"

"Viva Cheno Cortina! Death to our enemies!" the men yelled back.

Cheno turned to Tomas. "Take some men and free the prisoners. If you find Shears, kill him." Cheno gave the flag back to Tomas. "Put it back in your saddle bag," he added, touching Tomas' shoulder gently, a friendly smile in his face.

Tomas grumbled something, but nodded in agreement, he put the flag in his saddle bag, then he turned around, signaled a group of men and they all walked toward the jail.

Cheno walked over to talk to Alejo Vela. "Alejo, take several men with you. You know where to find Morris, punish him as he deserves. Show him the same mercy he showed his victims. Once you are done with him, find Billy Neale and treat him as he treated your cousins. Remember, no plundering and no harm should be caused to innocent people."

"I'll remember," Vela answered a severe look in his face. He signaled a group of men and they walked toward the Miller Hotel located at the corner of Elizabeth and Thirteenth Streets.

"Cheno, what should we do now?" Ceferino Morales asked.

"We are going to Werbiski's store and get guns and ammunition for our men. Many of them are armed only with machetes and knives. They won't be able to defend themselves if we are attacked." Cheno answered, walking as he talked, crossing the dusty street toward the store, followed by the rest of the men.

Once there, Cheno knocked on the solid oak door. It opened with a squeak. Antonieta, Werbiski's wife, stepped into the opening, shaking nervously, crying.

"Cheno," she said her voice trembling, fear in her eyes, "my husband and I have always treated Mexicans respectfully and honestly. Please don't harm us." She covered her eyes with both hands, sobbing loudly.

"Sssh, Tonita, calm yourself. This is not a night for more Mexican tears." Cheno replied opening his arms and hugging her gently, soothingly. "Call your husband; we are here for honest business."

After the guns and ammunition had been distributed among the men. Cheno paid the one hundred silver pesos that he was asked for.

"Thank you, Alejandro," Cheno said to Werbiski. "You are an honest man. Tell everyone that honest and fair people, like you, have nothing to fear from us."

"What's that noise," Judy, a recently arrived whore from New Orleans, asked Morris as she woke from sleep in his room in the Miller Hotel.

"Bah, don't bother. Those stupid Mexicans still celebrating their independence day. They are as noisy as they are useless," Morris replied turning over in the bed, attempting to go back to sleep. But the sound of booths and spurs rushing up the stairs alerted him of the imminent danger. He jumped up trying to get to his gambling coat, where he had his gun. Before he could get to it, a violent kick crushed the door lock. Through the wide open door several Mexicans walked in.

"What do you want?!" Morris yelled, a cold sweat running down his hands and forehead.

"We want to gamble," one of the Mexicans answered coldly, walking toward Judy, his spurs squeaked in the wooden floor. He took her clothes, throwing them to her. "Get dressed, guerita and get out of here, quickly."

"Jefe, esta buena la guerita," Morris heard one of the Mexicans saying. "Why don't you let us get a piece of her?"

"Callate, estupido," the man who had addressed Morris, answered. "You heard Cheno's. orders. No harm will be done to innocents."

On hearing Cheno's name, Morris felt a cold chill run through his back. A second later, though, he felt that he had recovered his gambling coolness.

"You said that you want to gamble," Morris said to the man who seemed to be the leader of the Mexicans. "What kind of gambling are you thinking about?"

"We'll play to the highest card," the Mexican answered.

"I see, and what are we betting?"

"The way you are going to die."

"How is that?"

"You see, if you get the lowest card we'll kill you slowly and in pain."

"What will happen if I get the highest card?"

"I'll be sure that you die quickly."

"You don't give me a chance!"

"Did you give it to your victims?" the Mexican snapped back. "Choose a card!"

Adolphus Glaevecke awoke to the noise of gunfire and the yelling of Cortina's name. He immediately knew he was in trouble. He dressed, grabbed the holster with his gun and rushed toward the jail. When he arrived, he was gasping for air. He knocked on the heavy door and, once inside he found Robert J. Johnston, the jailer and Viviano Garcia, one of Sandoval's assistants.

"Cortina's men are here and I'm afraid for no good!" Glaevecke shouted. "We need to notify Shears as soon as possible."

Before Johnston or Garcia could answer, the noise of men coming made them jump toward their rifles. They'd no sooner armed themselves when heavy blows pounded against the door.

"Who is out there?" Johnston asked, cocking his rifle.

"Abre la puerta, cabron," someone yelled back.

"We'll open when your chingada madre comes naked," Garcia replied, in Spanish, pointing his rifle toward the door.

Glaevecke, sweating heavily, pulled his gun out and cocked it. When he pointed it at the door, he was shaking so hard, he barely was able to hold it steady.

Gunshots blew the door lock away. Two Mexicans pushed the heavy door that gave way, swinging wide open. Garcia and Johnston fired their rifles almost simultaneously. The two Mexicans, who had pushed open the door, fell, but others behind them fired back. Glaevecke watched in horror as Johnston and Garcia fell. He fired his gun before rushing toward the back door, leaving a trail of urine behind him.

Once outside, Glaevecke, ran as fast as he was able, crossing Elizabeth St, turning on Levee Street to knock at Jerry Galvan's store. As soon as the door opened, he jumped in, barring the door.

"Cortina's men just killed Johnston and Garcia, and now they are coming after me," Glavecke said to Galvan, gasping for air.

"Although I don't like you and your methods," Galvan replied, "You may stay here. I don't approve killing. I know Cheno won't harm me or my family." Glavecke felt the coolness of Galvan's stare. "And don't attempt anything treacherous while you are here. Come inside, let's have some coffee," Galvan added.

After killing Morris, Vela and his men strode down dusty Elizabeth Street toward Neale's house, a beautiful wooden structure, with a well groomed garden at the entrance. As soon as the Mexicans opened the garden gate, someone opened fire from the house. Cipriano Vela, Alejo's younger brother, yelled and fell to the ground, dying almost immediately.

Watching his brother being shot to death, Alejo felt a sudden rage. "Fire!" he yelled, pulling his gun and shooting along with the rest of the Mexicans. Someone grunted in pain from the porch of the house. Alejo and the rest of the men ran to the porch and found young Billy Neale lying on the floor, blood running through his mouth, nose and chest. He was dead.

"Oh, God," a woman sobbed from inside of the house.

Alejo stood up, walked into the house. On opening the front door, he saw William Neale, his wife and two children all hugging each other, sobbing loudly and looking scared.

"They killed Cipriano, your brother," Victoriano Ramirez told Alejo. "They deserve to die. They have to pay for his death."

Alejo looked at the Neale family, and then turned to Victoriano. "Enough people have died today. We aren't assassins. We don't kill innocent people. Let's go and bury my brother. Let them bury their son," he said in a cold voice. The darkness of the night prevented all from seeing a tear running down his cheek.

The sound of galloping horses, shooting, and yelling, awoke Shears.

"Free the prisoners!" "Free the Mexicans!" "Viva Cortina," the shouts rang from outside, immediately clearing his mind. He leaped to his feet, dressed and ran toward the jail. Before he could get there he saw that a band of Mexicans was already there. He realized that there was nothing he could do to help his deputy or to prevent the prisoners from being liberated. Now it was his life that was in danger. If the Mexicans caught him they would show him no mercy: he had never shown any for them.

A sudden sensation of terror struck him. He ran, thinking of nothing else, but a place to hide. As he ran through 12th Street he saw a bakery, dashed inside and looking around in desperation. Toward the back was an old bakery oven, no longer in use. He crawled into it, closing the metallic door behind him. Sobbing and shaking, he breathed in an unpleasant odor. The weight in his pants and the sudden humidity in the adobe oven, made him aware that his sphincters had relaxed.

"We haven't been able to find Glaevecke or Shears," Tomas informed Cheno a bit later. By then they were installed in what used to be the headquarters of Fort Brown. "Glaevecke was at the jailhouse, but was able to run away. He must be hiding in one of the houses in the vicinity. Should we look for him house by house?"

"No, innocent people live there and I don't want to put them in danger," Cheno replied. "But have our men patrol the streets. If anyone sees him or Shears, kill them on the spot. No mercy for them."

"No one has seen Shears at all. The door to his house is open, but nobody is in there. He just disappeared. Well, the sun is now rising," Tomas added. The roosters happily crowed, welcoming the new day.

"Cheno, some people from Matamoros and Brownsville want to talk to you," Vela notified Cheno a while later. His voice was cold. "General Carbajal, Miguel Tijerina, Iturria, Stillman and some others. They say that they are coming in peace."

Cheno, who was sitting at a table eating breakfast, used a flour tortilla as spoon, took some of the scrambled eggs with hot sauce, chewing it, slowly, the hot sauce made him sweat. "Let them in. Let's hear what they have to say," he said after swallowing and taking a sip of his coffee with cinnamon. He used the back of his right hand to wipe some of the sweat from his forehead.

"Cheno, what are you doing?" General Carbajal asked as soon as he and the rest of the people were introduced. "You have created an international problem. Mexico already has enough problems with the imminent invasion by some of the European countries. And now this! Do you want to restart the war with the United States?"

"I'm not trying to start any war," Cheno replied, angrily. "I've chosen to become a citizen of the United States. My ranch, my wife, my family are here. But, there is no justice for us. Our land, our property, our freedom have been taken away." He pointed toward Iturria, San Roman and others. "And you have done nothing about it. You have done nothing to restore our dignity, our pride. This is our land, and we are being treated as if we were invaders. In our land!"

His green eyes flashed, his red beard trembling along with his jaw. Cheno pointed then to Carbajal. "You General, you are the one who has come with an army. For what? To fight your own people? To fight those who are seeking Justice? To fight on the side of those who have humiliated our people, who have killed our people, who have robbed us, who have forced us to abandon our properties?"

"Cheno, we can understand your anger," Stillman intervened. "But the way you and your men are acting is the wrong way. Sneaking into town, killing people in the middle of the night, taking an entire American town hostage, will not accomplish what you are looking for." His blue eyes, usually cold, seemed friendly and warm to Cheno.

85

"He is right," Tijerina said. "And you are right too. No one can say that you are not speaking the truth." He smiled to Cheno. "You have taught us all a lesson. Your point has been made."

"Cheno what you have done here is courageous," Carbajal intervened again. "But now for the sake and safety of everybody you and your men should leave."

Cheno frowned, caressing his beard, pondering it all. "I believe that you are right," he said after a few seconds, standing up. "But we'll stay alert. It must be clear that we'll not tolerate anymore injustice against the weak and humble."

A couple of hours later, Cheno and his men left Brownsville. This time they rode slowly, in a dignified manner, proud and sitting tall in their saddles. Seeing them leaving, the townspeople went out, most of them cheering and waiving, others walking along with them, feeling their dignity restored and thankful for it.

Cheno went to his ranch, where his mother Estefana, his wife Rafaela and his brothers and sisters were waiting for him. Once there, Cheno asked Chema to write a manifesto in Spanish and English explaining the reasons for his actions. Chema agreed and started to work on it, almost immediately. Sabas, although upset, had agreed with their mother that he wouldn't argue with Cheno, so he just hugged him and wished him good luck. Rafaela happy to see her husband, hugged and kissed him .After explaining to his family the reasons for his actions, Cheno retired early, along with Rafaela.

CHAPTER 13

Mayor Powers, pressed by Glaevecke, Kenedy, Shears and others called for a meeting at City Hall in the Market Square. Among those invited were Iturria, San Roman, Stillman and all prominent citizens from Brownsville. Servando Canales, a well- known member of the Conservative Party in Mexico, General Carvajal, the Tijerina brothers and other wealthy merchants form Matamoros, were also present.

On watching them, Stillman could sense that most were nervous, some of them anxious and others, like Glaevecke, were really scared. Shears, although acting tough, was sweating, in spite of being a gorgeous, fresh fall morning. Stillman almost smiled; they had reasons to be afraid of Cortina. He noticed that only Iturria and San Roman seemed to be calm. On whose side were they?

"Cortina is dangerous." Glaevecke was the first to talk. "Like the rascal he is, he has sneaked in the middle of the night and killed our friends and neighbors." He stood up, raising his right arm, his fist closed. "We must put a stop to it! Cortina must be punished." He was loud and harsh, he swept his arm down to add emphasis to his words.

"Although ill advised, Cortina's actions are comprehensible. We must accept that lawlessness has become rampant in Brownsville and punishment has not been applied fairly to everyone. We have witnessed undue tolerance for criminal behavior from some. Among them, some of those that were punished by Cortina's." Iturria said, his voice sounded calm but firm.

"Are you accusing anyone in particular?" Shears growled.

"I'm just stating a fact," Iturria snarled back.

"We ain't here to discuss Cortina's motives," Kenedy intervened. "But to plan our defense and prevent future attacks." He looked around to everyone. "I've made sure that the Governor is properly informed about the events," he flashed a confident smile. "I'm sure he will send at least the rangers to help in our defense. Meanwhile, we must develop a plan of action."

"We'll start by barricading the streets and place a permanent guard to prevent Cortina from entering the City by surprise." Powers said

"That's a good start, but not enough," Kenedy said. "We must attack and either capture him or be sure that he leaves the country and never returns. That's the only safe way. My men are ready, but we'll need some other volunteers. A four pound cannon from my steamboat El Ranchero is at your disposal. Would the people from Matamoros be willing to join us?" He asked looking at General Carvajal.

General Carvajal rubbed his moustache, pensive for a few seconds, before answering. "We'll send sixty men and a ten pounds cannon," he replied. "Most of the merchants from Matamoros also consider Cortina's actions dangerous for the peace between our countries."

"I agree with that," Canales said. "Cortina and men like him must be stopped."

"I believe that we should first talk to Cortina. Some of his actions might appear to be wild to some of you. But I assure you that he is as reasonable as anyone here," San Roman intervened.

"Whose side are you?!" Shears yelled. "He is a ruthless assassin!" Saliva poured out as he spoke.

Like a rabid dog, Stillman thought, feeling disgusted.

"We all know that there are solid reasons for what Cortina did," San Roman snapped back. "You, better than anyone here, know that." He added, pointing at the Marshall.

Shears jumped out of his chair his fists clenched. He was stopped and held by Sheriff Brown and others before he could harm San Roman. .

"Gentlemen, gentlemen!" Powers said, raising his voice. "We aren't here to fight each other, but to plan how to protect the town from future attacks."

"Cortina has killed and robbed our friends and neighbors. He must be punished with all the rigor of the law," Glaevecke intervened. "Alexander," he turned to Werbiski. "Are you going to press charges for the stolen goods from your store?"

"He paid in gold for everything he took," Werbiski answered. "I accuse him of nothing. As a matter of fact he asked me to tell you that…."

"We don't care to hear whatever he might have said," Glaevecke roared before Werbiski could finish. "Are you trying to defend him?"

"He might be wild in some of his actions. But, he is not a ruthless man. On the contrary, more than once he has proven that he cares for the common people," Werbiski replied.

"I can't believe it!" Shears snapped in. "Now, it turns out that the sneaky assassin is a hero. Perhaps, we should join him," he added in a sarcastic tone.

"Of course not," Stillman intervened for the first time. "But we must be cautious, otherwise we could, indeed, make him a hero. First, we must prevent future attacks, so, I propose to support Mayor Powers and Mr. Kenedy in their plans. But also, San Roman is right. A commission should go and talk to Cortina. That way we can learn about his plans." He looked around as he spoke, assessing everyone's reaction to his words.

"Does everyone agree?" Powers asked.

"Well," he added after everyone nodded in agreement, "who is going to be in charge of organizing the barricades and the plan for the defense? Who will be in the commission to talk to Cortina?

"I'll take care of organizing the defense and the barricades," Kenedy said. "I hope General Carvajal will join the 'Brownsville Tigers.' We'll give Cortina a lesson." He added, looking grim and self satisfied.

He is too proud of himself, Stillman thought. I hope it's not Cortina who is giving us a lesson.

"While you take care of that, Iturria, San Roman, Stillman and whoever wants to join us, will talk to Cortina. I'm sure that there will be no more violence," Werbiski said.

A few days later, at San Jose ranch.

"Honest and honorable people have nothing to fear from me or any of my friends," Cheno told the members of the commission sent to talk to him. "Only those who have twisted the law to abuse peaceful and defenseless citizens have reason to fear our rage. But people like you can sleep in peace. We have no quarrel with you."

"Cheno, although you might have sound reasons for your actions, you must also understand that you have created a difficult situation for most of us," Iturria said. "If this is allowed to continue, it might get out of control. It could even start a war. There is a lot of tension already. But, you have the power to stop it. We have come here hoping that you'll be reasonable."

Cheno stood up, walked to the window and looked at the vaqueros that had camped in the ranch. "People from all over Texas and northern Mexico have come asking to join the fight." He pointed outside. "They are not only Mexicans, but also, Irish, Germans and Italians. It seems to me that they also have their solid reasons to wish to fight," Cheno answered, turning, he felt his face flushing.. "They have put their confidence on my shoulders. I can't ignore them now."

"We are well aware that there are plenty of people who might feel cheated and dispossessed. But, violence will only aggravate, not solve the problem," Stillman insisted, bending forwards in his chair as he spoke. "You can help by taking a step in the right direction, by stopping the violence. To continue on this path endangers everyone in the valley, including your family and specially those you claim to be defending."

Cheno looked at Stillman. Although he considered him to be a cold businessman, he felt that in this matter, he was sincere.

"Besides, Cheno, we must remember that there are more important issues brewing now. We must not forget that Mexico soon will be in need of all of its children. If you really wish to fight for a just cause you must keep your commitment to join the Mexican army and fight the European invaders." Tijerina reasoned.

"You have taught us all a lesson, which we won't forget. I assure you about that," Werbiski added.

"As I said before, honest and fair people, like you, have nothing to fear from us. Chema has put it in writing in the manifest that I'm sure you all have read," Cheno replied, then paused for a moment, looking again at them, before continuing. "We have tried to adhere to the new rules and live under American law and in spite of that, many of us find ourselves dispossessed of what used to be ours. But, I don't want to be the cause of more problems to my friends and neighbors and to show that I mean it, Rafaela and I will move to Mexico. We'll go in peace." He raised his right hand closing it, with his index finger pointing up. "But, if there is more injustice, if honest farmers of any nationality continue being treated unfairly, their land and property stolen, my men and I will return to defend them and punish those who deserve it. I swear to that!"

"That's the right attitude Cheno," Stillman said. "Keeping the peace must be our goal. You have made us all proud. Thank you." He stood up, as the rest did, all nodding in agreement, a satisfied look in their faces.

Two weeks later, Cheno and his vaqueros drove his cattle across the Rio Grande.

"Tomas, you will stay in charge of the San Jose ranch. If you have any problems, ask Chema or Sabas for guidance. Also, please take care of mama's needs in her ranch," Cheno told his good friend after the crossing.

"Don't worry Cheno, you know that I'll keep things in order until you come back," Tomas answered. 'You take good care of yourself, if you go and fight the European invaders." The creases in his face became deeper as he frowned, looking at the northern side of the river. "Look over there, Glaevecke and some of his friends are watching us. I wonder, what are they planning now to harm us? Those are like vultures, their presence means something bad is going to happen," he added, as he controlled his nervous horse.

That night at Glaevecke's house on Tenth St. a group of men gathered to discuss the events of the last days and the progress made in improving Brownsville's defenses. Besides Glaevecke, Miflin Kenedy, Jean Vela, Tomas Vazquez, Marshall Shears, and others were present.

"Well, it seems to me that the rascal of Cortina has gotten away with rampage and murder," Shears said in a rancorous voice.

"We watched them as they crossed his cattle to Mexico," Jean Vela said as he smoked his cigar. "It looked like they were crossing a lot of cattle. I wonder if all of it belongs to Cortina." He added, showing his rotten teeth in a cynical smile

"Everyone knows that he is a rustler," Vazquez interjected. "Perhaps he took cattle that doesn't belong to him."

"A rustler like him can't go unpunished," Shears said.

90

"But he is now on the Mexican side of the river. There is nothing we can do while he is out there. Besides people on both sides of the border see him as their hero, their defender," Sheriff Brown intervened. "It will be unwise to try something against him that would only restart the violence."

"That is true, but still we must give Cortina and his followers a lesson. If we allow Mexicans or any others to get away with actions like the one we just lived through, we'll be in serious trouble," Shears said. "We must show them who their master is."

"And, how would you propose to do that?" Kenedy asked.

"You said that the Governor is sending the Rangers. I propose to wait for them and once they are here, we'll go to San Jose ranch. If we can't punish Cortinas we can punish his followers. Shears stood up, tucked his hands in his pockets, looking satisfied. "Who knows?" he continued, "maybe, we could even recover your cattle and Mr. King's and some other stolen herd."

Kenedy smiled, "that's a good plan," he said. "I'll drink to that."

"Me too," Vazquez said, lifting his glass.

Three weeks later, on a cold and rainy November day, twenty- five men, in yellow raincoats, rode their horses through muddy Elizabeth St. Most were slender and strong. All of them, even the younger, had a mean and dreadful appearance. Some of them had scars carved into their dirty, unshaved, faces; while others, wore a black patch to cover a missing eye. Some were chewing tobacco and frequently spat it, it came out black with greenish spots, so thick that bounced when hitting the mud. Their leader was coughing in spurts and spitting blood. They rode slowly, knowing that the people were looking and already were fearful of them.

Papa, who are those men?" a child looking through a window asked.

"Those are the rinches, sent by the Governor to supposedly protect us from Cortina. But, considering what we are seeing, I wonder, who is going to protect us from them?" The man hugged the child close, as though shielding him from danger.

One month later, at Matamoros. Cheno and Rafaela had been invited to participate in a posada, a traditional celebration where Mexicans recall the struggle of Joseph and Mary to find a hostel before her imminent delivery. It was a cold night and after the traditional breaking of the piñata by the children, singing hymns and praying the rosary, Cheno was enjoying a hot champurrado with tamales along with several friends when Alejo Vela entered the house. As soon as Cheno saw him, he knew that something was wrong, It was obvious that he had been riding for a long distance, Alejo's jaws were tight his eyes wide open and although it was a cold night, his cheeks were pale.

Cheno, his eyes fixed in Alejo, put down the cup with champurrado and swallowed the piece of tamale already in his mouth.

"Cheno," Alejo said as soon as he approached. "I bring bad news." The room became silent, everyone turning at Alejo. Rafaela paled. An anxious look in her face.

"What is it?" Cheno asked.

"Glaevecke, Shears and the rinches attacked San Jose ranch. They have killed almost everyone, even women and children. They seized all the cattle, claiming that it was stolen." Alejo paused for a moment. "Tomas was taken prisoner and they are planning to hang him."

A murmur of disgust rose from the group. Cheno stood silent for a moment. He looked at Rafaela, whose eyes were fixed on him.

"Severo, bring my horse," he said to one of the members of the party. "Get the men ready, we are going to Brownsville."

"Cheno," Rafaela said, walking towards him and hugging him. "Please, be careful," she whispered in his ear. "I didn't bleed last month."

Cheno looked at her surprised. He smiled, happy with the news, kissed her, hesitated for a moment, then looked around and made a signal to Sabas to approach.

"Brother," Cheno said. "Please, take Rafaela with mama and take good care of her. You are going to be an uncle."

CHAPTER 14

It was a cold and damp night. The sea breeze swirled hard, making it difficult to ride against, even for those used to the harsh and ever- changing weather conditions in the fall along the Rio Grande Valley. Thunderbolts at the distance announced an upcoming storm and along with the rattling symphony of the mezquite and palm trees leaves it muffled the growl of the wild animals. Cheno and Alejo fought the dew, the mud and the wind, riding as hard as they could, on their way to where Cheno's men were camping. From there, they would go on to Brownsville to rescue Tomas from his captors.

After they had crossed a slippery and treacherous resaca, suddenly, they found themselves surrounded by mounted men. Lightning illuminated the half- naked bodies of the Indians who had closed in around them. The horses bucked and neighed when the reins tightened to a sudden stop.

"Comanches!" Alejo said. "We are cut off, there is no escape!"

Before they could react, they were dragged off their horses, thrown to the mud. Some of the Comanche quickly dismounted, holding Cheno and Alejo tight. Cheno tried to pull away and in the struggle, the necklace around his neck jumped out the collar of his shirt, catching the attention of one of the Comanches, who pulled it of from Cheno's neck. After looking at it, he grumbled something to the other Indians. They eased off their grip on Cheno and Alejo. Although still holding them, their grip was no longer forceful or painful. The Indian walked away and showed the necklace to their leader who had been watching the struggle from a distance.

The leader of the Comanche dismounted and walked toward Cheno, holding the necklace in his hand, his eyes fixed on Cheno.

"Where did you get this?" he asked, in Spanish, extending his arm and showing the necklace to Cheno.

"It was given to me by one of your chiefs sometime ago." Cheno replied

"This necklace identifies a Comanche chief," the Indian told them. "You must be the man we have heard of. There is a story of a Mexican in the Rio Bravo, who shared his food and gave horses to our people in need. It is repeated among us. I heard it at the Mission in Parras." He ordered the Indians to release Cheno and Alejo, who lifted their hats from the mud, brushed them off before putting them back on their heads.

The Comanche chief gave the necklace back to Cheno who took it and put it around his neck.

"We'll ride with you wherever you are going," the chief told them once they were all back on their horses.

The wind, the rain and the lighting increased. Feeling the heavy raindrops hitting his face Cheno felt strong and cheerful, he regarded the appearance of the Comanche and their attitude toward him as a good omen.

"It seems that you are getting ready for a fight," the Comanche chief said, once they arrived at the camp.

"Indeed," Alejo replied, "we are crossing the river, going to Brownsville and, if necessary, will fight to free our friends."

"We'll join you. Your enemies are our enemies. Your fight is our fight." The chief said emphatically.

Cheno turned his horse to face the Indian. "You are welcome to join our forces. Our cause is a good cause. But, you must understand that we offer only to share our food. We are not fighting for money, land or power. We fight for pride, respect and dignity, that's all."

"Are there better reasons for a warrior to die?" the Comanche asked, smiling.

Cheno looked at the Comanche and smiled back at him. "No, I can't think of one" he answered. Then he turned to Alejo. "Get the men ready. We are leaving immediately."

The following evening, Cheno and his men camped just outside of Brownsville. Cheno sent Alejo to talk to Mayor Powers and arrange for a meeting. Stephen Powers agreed. He, Captain Tobin, leader of the Rangers, Mifflin Kenedy, General Cavazos and several other prominent citizens from Brownsville and Matamoros, would meet with Cortinas at his camp at daybreak.

"Gentlemen," Cheno told them the following morning, "we don't want to cause trouble; all that we ask for is Tomas' freedom. As soon as he is with us, we'll leave in peace and no harm will be done." They were all sitting on the grass around a fire that had been lit for them by Cheno's men.

"Tomas Cabrera has been indicted for his part in the events that ended in the killing of several men," Tobin said. He coughed covering his mouth with a red handkerchief. "There are several witnesses and most important, he has confessed to Cassoos Sandoval. He will hang, as will you or anyone else who breaks the law. "His voice was harsh, guttural; his breathing difficult. Coughing made his speech intermittent.

Cheno felt a chill run up his back at Tobin's ghostly voice. He winced when Tobin spat blood, noticed his pale, emaciated, bloodless cheeks, his sunken, icy blue eyes, and the long nails with blue and swollen fingertips. The days of this man are numbered, Cheno thought, and for that reason, he realized that Tobin would be pitiless toward others' suffering.

"Besides, this time we are ready for you," Kenedy intervened. "If you care about your life and the lives of your men, you will leave peacefully today. Otherwise we'll crush you."

Cheno turned to face him. Kenedy's eyes, usually cheerful and friendly were cold and menacing. Cheno realized that Kenedy was not bluffing. They wanted a fight, they wished for it. Cheno's muscles tensed, his breathing became deeper. Although he was ready and willing to fight, a subtle sadness overcame him. Almost instinctively, he looked up. In the distance vultures were circling

. "Cheno," Mayor Powers said. "I assure you that Tomas will have a fair trial. There are people who will testify on his behalf. Most of us understand that there were reasons for the recent events."

Cheno noticed that Shears and Tobin looked at Powers with rancor.

"Tomas must be freed. Once he is with us we'll leave and there will be peace," Cheno said in a calm but firm voice, looking at Kenedy and Tobin. "If you want trouble, you'll get it. But, I want to make this clear, it is up to you. We'll wait until tomorrow night. If Tomas is not with us by then, we'll go and free him, by force, if necessary."

"You must understand that the Mexican government will not support you. We aren't interested in starting another war," General Cavazos said.

"No one wants a war. All that we are asking for is fair justice. If it is possible for you, wealthy and powerful, to ignore the fact that people who are your neighbors, your friends,   are being robbed, humiliated, killed, and sent to jail for no reason. If you can ignore it and look the other way, pretending that nothing is happening, we can't and we won't. We hear their clamor, we feel their pain and we'll defend them." Cheno replied. "But we don't want war. Fairness and justice for all is all that we ask for." His cheeks flushed, his eyes sparkled, his back straightened as he spoke.

"No one who is friendly to the Indians deserves respect," Tobin said rudely, pointing to the Comanche and getting up, starting to walk away. "What we came to say is already said. Good bye. Next time the bullets will do the talking." He coughed and spat a coagulum that bounced on the ground. The rest of the men stood up and followed him.

That night, Cheno took a walk outside the camp. The horses were pasturing freely. The grass is high even in this season, he thought. This valley is great for cattle. Memories flowed. He remembered how Tomas had taught him, when a child, how to ride a pony. He saw himself as a teen learning from Tomas how to tame a mustang. He saw Tomas showing him the secrets of the Valley, how to capture a wild horse, catch a run away bull. In his imagination, he also saw Rafaela smiling at him. She was with child, his child.

Cheno smiled. He hoped the people of Brownsville would be sensible so that he could leave peacefully. He stopped, took a deep breath and looked toward the town, not far away.

Through the mist and fog he glimpsed torches moving fast. He heard people shouting. There was gunfire.

"What could that be?" Alejo asked as he joined Cheno.

"I don't know. It sounds like a riot," Cheno replied.

"Look, a couple of riders are leaving town and galloping in this direction." Alejo said.

"Let's wait for them and we'll find out," Cheno said.

As they watched, the riders galloped into camp and continued toward where Cheno and Alejo were standing.

"Cheno!" one of them shouted as soon as they were close. "You must hurry up. They are about to lynch Tomas!"

"What?!" Cheno yelled. "How is that? What is going on?"

"Shears, Glaevecke, Sandoval and the rangers have created a riot and they are on their way toward the jail. They are yelling for Tomas to be hanged. They have Sheriff Brown surrounded at his house. There is nothing he can do to stop them. You must come now!" The man yelled back.

"Let's go to the horses!" Cheno yelled

Since all of them were experienced and seasoned vaqueros, it took them only a few minutes to get and saddle their horses. Precious minutes, however. Although they galloped at full speed, by the time they reached town, past the humble jacales with walls made of wood sticks and roof of palm leaves, the better built adobe houses, and finally, the solid wood and brick houses with gardens in their front yards, the homes of the wealthy. By the time they reached Market square, Brownsville was silent. Gone were the rioters, the torches, the yelling. Only the whistle of an owl and the rattling of the palm trees were heard. The fog and mist made Brownsville look like a sepulchral, ghostly town. The doors were closed, no light shone from any house. The streets were deserted, only a few skinny, street dogs circled around a body lying in front of the market building.

Cheno dismounted, slowly walked toward the body covered with mud and blood. A rope still around his neck and another one around the ankles. Flies circled around the corpse. Cheno recognized Tomas. He knelt, lifted the head of his friend, the head moved, but the body didn't follow, it was connected to the body only by the skin. Sandoval's horses had almost separated it.

Carefully, Cheno lifted the shoulders and let them rest on his knees, while he caressed the unshaven deeply wrinkled face of the old man. He lowered his head and sobbed. He looked up and yelled a loud, savage, pain- filled yell that resonated and was heard in Matamoros and throughout the entire Valley. Thunderbolts echoed Cheno. The rest of the men, some of them weeping, kept a respectful distance.

"Cheno." Alejo approached. "What should we do now?"

"We should put the torch to the town. We must avenge Tomas," someone said.

"No," Cheno said, tenderly putting Tomas' body on the ground and getting up. "Most of the townspeople are innocent." He signaled to some men to approach him. "Be careful with him," Cheno told them. "Take him to El Carmen. Be sure his body is well washed and cleansed and he is shaven." Cheno turned to another man. "You, go and find Father Nicholas. We'll have mass and give Tomas a Christian burial."

Cheno started to walk to his horse when he suddenly stopped and would have fallen if Alejo hadn't caught him. Cheno put his head on Alejo's chest and sobbed bitterly.

Someone found a carriage to transport Tomas' body. Cheno and his men left town in a slow procession. As they crossed in front of the solid wood and brick houses with gardens in their front yards, those houses remained in the dark. When they reached the adobe houses, these were lit and people came out holding candles and walked slowly on the side of the carriage. Women with their heads shawled, men holding their palm sombrero on their hands. They whispered the rosary as they walked. When they reached the humble jacales with walls made of wood stick and roofs of palm leaves, people came and covered Tomas body with wild flowers.

CHAPTER 15

Few days after Tomas' funeral, the Cortina's had a family meeting at El Carmen Ranch. Besides the members of the family, Charles Stillman, Francisco Iturria and Jose San Roman were present. They had been invited by Estefana and Sabas. Except for the guests, all members of the Cortinas's family were dressed in black. They considered Tomas a member of the family

"Cheno," Sabas opened the discussion. "Your men have besieged Brownsville and are seizing the mail," his voice raised "That's madness! You have started a war with no chances of winning it!" He calmed down a bit, looked at Cheno. What is it that you want?"

"We didn't start it." Cheno replied holding Sabas' look. "It was started by those who have taken advantage of the circumstances. Although Mexico was defeated and this land is now part of the United States, there is a Treaty that gives us, those who have been here for over a century; rights. It must be respected by all, not only us." He smiled. "And we are not seizing the mail, we are only being sure that there is no misinformation sent outside. Once we are sure of it, we allow it to pass."

"Well, that's true. I'll give that to you. But, as far as the treaty is concerned, we can say that we have been treated fairly." Sabas said.

"Have we?" Cheno said in a sarcastic tone, moving forwards to add weight to his words. "Tomas was assassinated. Mama was paid one dollar for the property where Brownsville has been built. Besides, I'd like to remind you that when I say 'us' I'm including our friends, neighbors, people with whom we have shared so many things for so long. People with whom we have grown up, whose families have been here for over one hundred years. Whose grandparents, along with ours, tamed this valley."

"You must understand that the deal with your mother, Dona Estefana, was a fair deal" Stillman intervened. "If we haven't done what we did. It would have been difficult for your family to keep your properties, including San Jose Ranch."

Cheno grinned. "And as result of it, you have made hundreds of thousands of dollars."

Stillman flushed.

"Cheno, the deal was approved by all of us, except you." Sabas said.

"That is an affair of the Cortina's family, San Roman intervened. "You might want to discuss it later among yourselves. But, for now, let's concentrate in the reason for this meeting." He paused for a moment, and then looked at Cheno. "Most of us are trying to understand the reasons you have taken this path. There might be a justification for it. But, I agree with Sabas, you have no chances of winning."

"Cheno," Iturria said. "Despite of all of your efforts, the information that the authorities in Austin and Washington have received is that you are raising an army with the purpose of restarting the war to bring Texas back to Mexico." He paused and looked at the others in the room. "All of us here know that it isn't true. But, as a result, you are now considered a dangerous outlaw and the consequences of all of this will not be good, especially for those you claim to defend."

"The Rangers are already making sure that people understands that there will be dire consequences for those who support you." San Roman said.

Cheno got up, walked and looked through the window. Among hundreds of monarch butterflies, he saw some of the men who followed him, many of them dressed in plain white cotton shirt and pants. So different among themselves, there were Italians, Germans, Irish, Mexicans, Indians, mostly Catholics but also some Mormons, men who under other circumstances would have fought each other. A good number of them had traveled many miles to join this fight.

"What about them?" he asked, pointing to the men. "They also have reasons to be here, to fight." He turned around and faced those in the room. "Should we ignore them? All that we are asking for is fairness in the application of the law. Is that too much? We have appealed to Governor Houston, until we hear from him we'll continue fighting. We didn't want it; this struggle wasn't started by us. But I'm certain that it is worth the sacrifice we are making." As he talked, he raised his voice to add weight to his point. .

"What about Rafaela?" Estefana asked. "She is with child, your child."

Cheno paled, felt a sudden tightening in his chest. He turned and looked at Rafaela, who gazed back at him tenderly. He walked toward her, kneeled and put his head on her lap. She caressed his hair, lovingly, motherly.

"Oh God," he said, "I love you and this child so much. This struggle is also for both of you and all the children of our friends. I hope that you understand. I don't want to be the cause of harm for any of you."

Gently, she lifted his chin, looked at him, tears shining in her eyes. Through her eyes Cheno felt her passion, her love. She smiled at him, a tender, sweet, but sad smile.

"You are Cheno Cortina, the man I love," she said, almost in a whisper. "Since we were children I watched you always taking the side of the weak, the less fortunate. You have never turned your back and pretended that a misdeed wasn't done. For that reason, I learned to love you and I'll always will." She raised her voice so everyone could hear. "You couldn't turn your back now. If you do so, you would be so gloomy."

"Why do you always have to get involved in someone else's business?" Sabas asked, getting more upset. "Let them defend themselves, let them take care of their own deeds."

"You should look out for yourself Cheno, "Iturria said, "with the land owned by your family, the present and the future are yours. That's if, as Sabas says, you look after your own business and let others take care of theirs."

"Business is business. People must learn to take care of themselves." Stillman said. "Yes, some times injustice happens in the process. It is something that we must learn to live with. We should strive for honesty and fairness. But there always be those who win and those who loose. That's a fact of life. "He paused for a moment. "There are laws, and law must be respected. There is no real reason for this mess."

"We are now citizens of United States," Sabas said, "and we must now live by its laws."

"Listen to your soul, son," Estefana said.

"Yes, my love, listen to your soul," Rafaela said. "I'll support and love you, whatever you decide."

Cheno looked at her tenderly. His eyes became hard as he turned to face the others.

"Yes, we are now citizens of the United States", Cheno said. "God knows that we have tried to live by its laws. And is true that as long as we are submissive and look the other way when our neighbor is forced out of his property, or when a misdeed is done to one of our friends, then we'll be fine. But I can't do that. I can't pretend that our neighbors have not been forced out, legally robbed. Yes there are laws, and all that we want is to be treated as what we are: Citizens! That's why we have appealed to the Governor." He paused, look at all the present, took a deep breath. "We'll continue with our struggle for justice until we hear from the Governor. I hope it will be favorable," he added.

Rafaela walked toward him, kissed him on the lips first then on the cheek, held his hands, smiling. "Cheno I'm only sorry that I'm not a man to follow you." She said.

"Although I don't agree with your decision, I'll always be proud of you," Estefana said walking toward him and putting her hand in Cheno's shoulder.

"Mama, Sabas, will you take care of her?" Cheno asked, holding his mother's hand while looking at Rafaela, "Chema has already said that he will join us."

"You have chosen a toilsome path and I'm sorry for that. But, the answer to your question is yes, you can be sure of that." Sabas answered.

"Although I also don't agree with your decision," Stillman said.

"I believe Pancho and Jose will join me in assuring that we'll do everything within our power to be sure that your mother, your wife and their properties will be safe." Stillman said.

Iturria and San Roman nodded in agreement.

A few days later, at Cheno's camp.

"Cheno, the men are getting hungry. I sent some men to get cattle. They went to Brown's ranch and got it." Alejo said.

"Be sure that we pay Brown a fair prize for his cattle," Cheno said, smiling. "Whatever our enemies say, we are not rustlers."

"I'll be sure of that," Alejo said. "We'll do every effort to keep this an honest fight. That's why people are risking supporting us."

"Cheno!" a rider approaching camp yelled.

"What is it?" Cheno asked as soon as the vaquero got close.

"I've been sent to warn you. They are coming for you. Kenedy's Tigers, the Rangers and men from the Matamoros militia, sent by General Carvajal will attack tonight. They have two cannons." the vaquero said as soon as he had dismounted.

"Is that so? I'm not surprised," Cheno said, smiling. "I knew they would try something like that sooner or later. It's better sooner. We'll give them a nice welcome." He slapped the vaquero's back.

That afternoon a heavy storm unleashed a pouring rain over the entire Valley. The resacas filled; the terrain became thick and muddy. By night fall though, the air was misty and moonlight shone through the remaining clouds. Cheno had ordered the fires on the camp to be lit, so they could be clearly seen from town. Hay dummies were strategically placed around the fire. Cheno ordered his men to hide on the shore meadows of the close by resacas. From there they could observe the camp and the town. When the night came they were able to watch the men leaving Brownsville advancing slowly, with mud up to their knees, those mounted, had to dismount and pull their horses. They were pulling a cannon that got stuck and after several attempts they couldn't move it. It was clear to Cheno that thanks to the moon light and the fire in Cheno's camp, the advancing men could see how what they thought were Cheno's men, sitting, probably eating, unsuspecting the imminent attack. They decided to leave the stuck cannon behind and continued advancing with difficulty through the mud.

Once the advancing men considered that they were close enough to Cheno's camp, they set their second cannon and tried to fire it, but it failed, it seemed that the mist and the sea breeze prevented them from lighting it. Cheno could hear Kenedy ordering his men to start firing, but again, the breeze and mist prevented them from putting the lid to their muskets, and for others it seemed that they couldn't get the cartridges into their muskets. Few were able to fire.

"Now, don't be too rough with them," Cheno said to Alejo and Chema, trying not to laugh.

Caught by surprise the Brownsville men ran away in all directions. Slipping, jumping through the thick mud, leaving their guns, horses and mules behind. Cheno's men caught few prisoners and let the rest go, laughing at them.

"Cheno we got two cannons, horses, mules, guns and few prisoners, "Chema told Cheno once they were back at the camp. "What we should do with them?"

"Of course we'll keep the cannons and guns. Send the horses back" Cheno replied, holding a cup of hot coffee with goat milk. "Do any of our men know how to fire the cannons?"

"Yes, already some of the Italians and Irish are working on them." Chema said. "I'll be sure that the horses are sent back to town. What about the prisoners? Some of the men are threatening to shoot them."

"I personally will shoot anyone who harms any of them," Cheno said. "Bring the prisoners."

"Gentlemen," Cheno told the captured men once they were brought to him. "You are free to go. We want you and all the people in the Valley, to know that we mean no harm to those who are honest and fair." He paused, looking at each one of them. "Although you came here tonight with plans to kill us, we have nothing against you. Go home and remember that all of us are now American Citizens. We all have the same rights."

A few days later, a rider at full gallop approached the camp.

"Cheno, the Rangers have attacked Santa Rita to punish them for sending food and supplies to your men. They claim that they want to give a lesson that all will understand. Anybody who supports you will be severely punished. They are burning the jacales and killing anything that moves. We need your help immediately!" The vaquero said as soon as he was able to catch his breath.

"Let's go!' Cheno yelled. "Get your horses. Let's defend our people!"

By the time they arrived to the little village, they found that all the jacales were burning. Dogs, pigs, chicken, horses, bulls, cows and people were lying down bleeding, dead or injured. A child cried on the side of her dead mother. A coyote at the distance howled, echoing the child's cry. Vultures circled the town.

"They can't be far. Let's go after them and revenge our people!" Cheno yelled.

Knowing the terrain by heart and being expert trackers, Cheno's vaqueros soon caught the Rangers who were trying to get back to Brownsville. Cheno's men surrounded their enemies. Although the Rangers adopted a defensive position, they were unable to stand the brutal attack. They were defeated by Cheno's angry men. But this time, the vaqueros were blood thirsty, this time they didn't feel satisfied by just defeating their enemy, this time they wanted revenge. The few surviving Rangers were hanged, and to be sure that no one was alive, all the bodies were cut in pieces with machetes. It was a savage, bloody orgy.

"Cheno, we *must* put a stop to this butchery!" Chema yelled.

"Go ahead and try," Cheno replied coldly. "Besides they came to teach us a lesson. Let's shown them how well we've learned."

"This is not right," Alejo said. "We can't become like those we are trying to combat."

"How would you prevent these men from showing their anger?" Cheno said. "Until now we have been able to contain them. But I was afraid that sooner or later something like this would happen." He pulled out his gun and shot several times into the air.

"Enough!" He yelled, "Enough, put your machetes back to the holders. Those men are dead! Save your anger for those who will be coming to revenge them."

"You saw what they did to the people in Santa Rita!" One of the vaqueros yelled.

"Yes, we all saw that. But we can kill them only once!" Cheno yelled back. "Go back to your horses. Let's go now and try to help the survivors at Santa Rita."

"At least we are now in control of the entire Valley," Alejo said as they were riding back.

A flock of roadrunners and another of wild turkeys ran ahead of them. In the distance Cheno noticed a puma getting ready to catch its prey. Memories flooded. He saw himself as a child and as a teen being taught by Tomas and the other vaqueros the secrets of the wild life in the Valley. He wished he could go back to those peaceful, innocent days. He had to force himself back to the present.

"We still have a lot to do," he said putting his horse to a gallop.

Chema and Alejo followed him.

CHAPTER 16

At Stillman's home on Elizabeth St. as usual in the early spring, the sea breeze was gentle and refreshing. That, along with the orange, purple, red and yellow colors of the sunset, the singing of hundreds of birds in the trees and the bright hues in the wings of thousands of butterflies, on their way back north, should have been enough to make it a spectacular evening, pleasant to feel, to be alive. But Charles Stillman, standing at his porch while waiting for his guests, barely noticed any of this. He was upset and uncommonly for him, he felt anxious. Both of the countries he loved were on the verge of dire social turmoil and he was afraid that his business and all he'd worked for would collapse as a result.

One by one his guests for the evening showed up. Francisco Iturria, Jose San Roman, Sabas Cortina, Mifflin Kenedy, Pastor Chamberlain, Stephen Cowen, Captain Tobin of the Rangers, Marshal Shears, Sheriff Brown and all the prominent citizens from Brownsville and Matamoros, all showed up.

"There is serious trouble in both countries," Stillman said once all were comfortable at the interior garden of his house. Cognac and imported wines filled their crystal glasses and for those who wanted them, Cuban cigars were offered. "French, English and Spanish troops have occupied Veracruz. These countries are threatening to invade Mexico, if their demands for prompt payment from the Mexican government are not satisfied." He paused for a moment, making sure that everyone was listening, and then took a deep, slow breath. "Besides that, my informers in Mexico and Europe tell me that the conservatives are not only supporting the invasion, they are already searching for an European prince willing to rule Mexico. The Empire of Mexico."

"That is exactly what they need," Pastor Chamberlain said, cheerfully. "They are a weak, lazy and degenerate race. They need a strong and firm hand to govern them." He paused to sip his cognac. "Democracy is not for everyone...."

"But now the Mexican will need to use Tampico and Bagdad as an outlet. That will be good for our business," Iturria said, interrupting Chamberlain.

"It would be, if it weren't' for Cheno. He is in control of the entire Rio Grande Valley. Nothing can be done if he doesn't allow it," San Roman said.

"It's shameful, that we have allowed him to take control." Kenedy said. "Our river boat company is losing money thanks to him. Everyone is afraid of losing their merchandise if it's moved. Passengers are also scarce. White people are afraid of Cortina's men and Mexicans of the rangers," he added before putting a cigar in his mouth and biting it.

Stillman noticed a grimace on Tobin's face.

"That's not all," Stillman said before Tobin could reply to Kenedy's last remark. "On our side of the border, it's now clear that there will be secession. The South won't relinquish its right to hold slaves. They are an important and necessary part of its economy."

"But, would the federal government in Washington allow for peaceful separation?" Sabas asked.

"If it's necessary we'll go to war, and we'll win it," Shears said.

"If there is war, as it seems that there will be," Stillman said, "the south has a better army, but as we all know, the north will control the sea. We have already talked about that."

"Cotton will become more precious than gold," Iturria said.

"It will be the winning card for the South," San Roman said.

"But, with the North controlling the sea, it will become necessary to have an outlet for it," Sabas said.

"And the logical one is the Port of Bagdad, right here," Kenedy smiled.

"King has already established the contacts and routes to bring the cotton through his ranch to Laredo, Roma or Brownsville," Stillman pointed out.

"And from there to Bagdad using our river boats," Kenedy's smile broadened.

"We have already granted your boats the use of the Mexican flag," General Cavazos said. "Business will be good for all."

"But, let's remember. Cheno controls the entire valley," Tijerina said, a touch of irony in his voice.

"Cheno's war must come to an end. He must go." Stillman drew himself up and looked at the others, showing his determination.

"But his motives are just," San Roman said, timidly.

"It's not a matter of Justice," Iturria intervened. "His motives might be just, but we must be sensible. He has no chances of winning."

Kenedy, Shears and Tobin nodded.

"Fortunately for us," Stillman said, "the newspapers in Corpus Christi, San Antonio, Austin, Houston and Washington have greatly exaggerated the problem. They are saying that Cortina has an army large enough to invade and force Texas back to Mexico."

"But we know that's not true," Sabas said.

"Yes, but thanks to those rumors, it won't be difficult to convince the Governor to send troops and additional rangers. Cheno must be defeated!" Stillman said, raising his voice, moving his right hand downward to add emphasis.

"We all agree with that," Iturria said. "I propose that we all sign a letter to the Governor asking for Federal troops and more rangers."

"I support that," San Roman said.

All present nodded in agreement.

"Although Cortina has the support of the common people in Matamoros, my troops will fight him on the Mexican side, "General Cavazos said. "He is a menace to everyone's business."

"What about you Sabas?" Kenedy asked.

"I agree," Sabas whispered, grimacing as he spoke.

A couple of weeks later, Brownsville people observed Federal soldiers in tidy blue uniforms, marching through town. They entered through Elizabeth St. and marched to the beat of drums until they reached the abandoned Fort Brown, just across the river. One hundred and fifty mounted soldiers and fifty artillery men formed the group.

Mayor Stephen Powers, accompanied by General Cavazos and all prominent citizens from Brownsville and Matamoros greeted Major Samuel Heintzelman, commander of the Federal troops.

That evening Stillman offered a welcome reception to Major Heintzelman and his officers.

"This is a far cry from what a certain H. C. Miller swore in Austin," Heintzelman said to Stillman and others during the party.

"What's that?" Stillman asked.

"Well, the man swore that Cortina had not only taken the town but that he had passed all able men to the sword," Heintzelman replied.

Stillman felt a knot tightening in his belly. He noticed how Iturria and San Roman grimaced in disgust.

"Cortina might be a rascal, but he is not an assassin," Iturria said.

"It really doesn't matter," Heinztelman said. "His actions have been serious enough to cause us to be ordered here. Soon, we'll engage him and we'll be sure he is no longer a threat to peaceful life here."

"On our way here, we noticed that most of the ranches have been burned, plundered," Captain Ricketts, commander of the artillery said. "I thought Cortina was fighting to protect their rights."

"And indeed, he is," San Roman said. "You saw the ranger's favorite method for keeping peace."

"Law and order must be maintained at any cost," Glaevecke said.

"Rascal behavior by the rangers will end once their new commander arrives," Heinztelman said.

"Who is him?" San Roman asked.

"John 'Rip' Ford" Heinztelman answered.

"Well, he is someone who would love to restart the war with Mexico," Stillman said, "but, he is a fair, firm, disciplined and above all, an honest man."

"A doctor and a lawyer," Iturria said, "he will be welcome."

"How is it that you know so much about him?" Ricketts asked.

"He was here before, with Taylor's army." San Roman explained.

Meanwhile at Cheno's camp, at the edge of the river, close to El Carmen ranch, most of the men tended to their horses, others cleaned their weapons, some played their guitars and sang high-pitched, cheerful sounding songs about broken hearts and unreciprocated love.

"If a stranger comes and looks at us now, he will think that we are at peace," Chema said smiling, pointing to the men.

"Unfortunately we are not," Cheno said. "You and Alejo will go to Brownsville and find out about the movements of the newly arrived army." He turned and looked at Alejo. "In particular, I'd like to know about their commander. Be careful and talk only to our friends there."

"We'll dress like common peasants," Chema said. "That way, hopefully, we'll not call the soldiers' attention to ourselves."

That evening, Chema and Alejo dressed in white cotton shirts and pants, huaraches on their feet, their heads covered with wide-brimmed hats made with rough palm fiber, walked through Market Square.

"Hey you!" Chema heard someone calling them. They turned and saw Alexander Werbiski.

"I need men to help me to move some heavy boxes at my store." Werbiski said. "Would you come and help?"

"Yes, we'll be glad." Alejo answered, sounding humble.

"Great. It's this way," Werbiski said walking toward his store.

"You are a couple of fools!" Werbiski said once they were inside his store. "Do you think that because you are dressed like common peasants no one will recognize you?" He shook his head nervously. "We have known each other since we were children." He exhaled, looking alternately to Chema then Alejo. "You were walking toward Jesus Sandoval. Had he seen you, you would be in jail. That is, if you were lucky."

"Thank you, Alejandro," Chema said, smiling and extending his left arm touching Werbiski's shoulder. "But we need to know about the soldiers and their plans."

"It's simple," Werbiski said. "Let's have a cup of coffee and I'll tell you what I know."

They were about to walk to the kitchen, located at the back of the store when commotion started on the street. People were rushing toward Market Square yelling. They sounded angry

"What it's going on?" Chema asked.

"Let's go and find out," Werbiski said, "but, be careful, keep your hats on and don't lift your heads."

They walked to Market Square and found that most of the town was already there. All were looking at a well dressed Mexican hanging from a large mesquite tree. On his chest, dangling from his neck was a piece a wood with a message written in Spanish. It was obvious that whoever wrote the message had used the dead's man blood. It was still dripping from his feet.

"SOPLON DE CORTINAS. (Cortinas's informer.)" Read the message.

Chema and Alejo immediately recognized Candelario de Luna, a rancher and good friend since childhood.

"Cabrones asesinos!" Chema whispered, his voice hoarse, rage filling him.

"Hijos de puta!" Alejo also whispered.

Captain Tobin, Jesus Sandoval and some of the Rangers stood a few steps in front of the hanged man, rifles ready to shoot whoever might try to cut Candelario's body down.

Soldiers arrived pushing people aside to let several officers through.

"Who did this?" the higher ranking officer asked angrily, pointing to the hanging man.

"That's Major Heinztelman, commander of the just arrived soldiers," Werbiski whispered to Chema.

"We did it," Tobin replied to the officer in a defiant tone.

"You already know Captain Tobin," Werbiski said to Chema and Alejo.

"On whose orders?" Heinztelman asked.

"Mine," Tobin answered, smugly.

Heinztelman went for his saber, but contained himself, jaws tight, fire coming from his eyes.

"We'll talk later," he said, making an obvious effort to stay calm. "Cut that man down and allow his family to take the body," he ordered the soldiers. "You go home in peace," he added addressing the townsfolk. "I'll see you in my quarters" he said to Tobin before turning around.

"That son of a bitch is going to make our job here difficult." Chema overheard Heinztelman talking to one of the officers.

Later, at Cheno's camp, Chema and Alejo sat with Cheno, sipping hot coffee with cinnamon and lots of brown sugar.

"Their commander seems to be an honest and sensible man," Chema said

"Indeed. Maybe we should try talking to him," Alejo added. "Who knows? Maybe he would understand our reasons and help us with the Governor."

Cheno smiled. "Do you really believe that?"

A flock of wild ducks landing stirred the seagulls on the river bank. The friends looked at the birds pensively.

"Werbiski told us that more Rangers are coming," Chema said. "They are getting a new commander. John Ford. Do you remember him? He was with Taylor."

"Yes, a good man. Hopefully he will control those savages," Cheno replied. "By the way, one of us must go and talk to Tomasita. She must

108

be assured that she and her children won't be abandoned now that Candelario is dead."

"The men are talking revenge," Alejo said.

"That will only cause more innocent blood to be spilled," Cheno said. "We'll not play their game. Ours is a just cause." He looked at the newly arrived ducks and the seagulls flying playfully. Suddenly, he felt optimist, smiled and looked at Alejo. "Maybe you are right. Let's arrange a meeting with their commander."

"Although Iturria, Stillman and San Roman signed the petition sent to the Governor, I'm sure they are also interested in a peaceful solution," Chema said. "They will help to arrange the meeting."

A few nights later, at Iturria's newly built home, Cheno, accompanied by Chema and Alejo met with Major Heinztelman and Captain Ricketts. Besides Iturria, Jose San Roman and Charles Stillman were also present. The curtains of the windows were down, but the new oil lamps illuminated the room well.

"I understand your reasons for engaging in this fight," Heinztelman said after Cheno had explained his reasons and the purpose of the struggle. "And I even think the Governor would understand and perhaps, even sympathize with you. But I doubt the political circumstances would allow him to do so." He paused for a moment, looked at Cheno, Chema and Alejo. "You must surrender." He paused again, passed his hand over his head, as though he were searching for the right words. "You will have a fair trial, that's the most I can offer you."

"Do you want us to surrender, just like that, accepting that nothing will change?" Alejo asked, in a loud voice, astonished. "What about all the innocent blood that has been spilled? What about all the ranchers thrown out of their properties?" His fiery black eyes looked at all the present, he looked anxious.

Cheno felt Alejo's pain. "We won't abandon our friends and their families. We have already taken enough. And, as a matter of fact, since the arrival of the rangers, things have worsened for our people. Most of us understand that, after Mexico's defeat, the circumstances for us have changed. We accept that fact and want to be Americans, like you. But many of your people don't feel the same way. There are those who believe that we are not created equal." He stared at Heinztelman and Ricketts.

"Your actions are the reasons for the coming of the Rangers and your actions are the reasons why we are now here," Captain Ricketts said. "It was you who brought this calamity to your people. That's why you must surrender."

"If we surrender," Chema said, "will the plunder of the ranches that have been here for decades, stop? Common Mexican peasants won't go to jail or be killed for no other reason than they look different?"

"We are soldiers, not politicians," Heinztelman said. "Our job is to bring peace. We are not here to judge your reasons. If you surrender you will prevent death, pain and suffering for those among you, that's all we can offer."

"I can tell that, like most of the American soldiers I've met, you are fair and honest men," Cheno said. "We understand that you have a job to do. We also have a responsibility to our people. To those who have put their trust on us. Thank you for accepting a meeting with us. We'll continue our fight."

"I hope you understand that you'll be facing professional soldiers now," Captain Ricketts said. "Even with the two small cannon in your possession, you are going to be crushed. Most of the casualties will be from your men. Avoid that and surrender. That's the reasonable path to take." His tone was friendly.

"Cheno, listen to them and be reasonable," Iturria intervened. "You have no chances of winning. Surrender."

The shriek of an owl outside sounded ominous.

"Have you thought about the consequences?" Stillman asked. "Your wife is with child. Are you willing to abandon them? Cheno be reasonable, surrender. We'll arrange a pardon with the Governor."

"This whole ordeal is unreasonable," Cheno said, in a friendly, but firm tone. "What is reasonable is to afford our people the protection we deserve by law. " He paused, stared at Stillman, Iturria and San Roman. "Yes, I have thought about the consequences, if we surrender now we'll live in shame, unable to look at our children straight in the eyes." Although he was feeling sad, Cheno smiled, shrugged his shoulders, and extended his right arm pointing toward the direction of the river. "Besides, we all know that if we surrender, those men will continue fighting, they have being doing so for sometime already." He turned and looked at the soldiers. "We'll meet again soon. All of us are aware that it won't be friendly." He stood up and extended his hand to Heinztelman and Ricketts.

CHAPTER 17

El Ebonal ranch a few miles north of Brownsville, it was the property of Francis M. Campbell, Cheno's friend and supporter. The sun rose while roosters happily crowed celebrating the arrival of a new day. Chema, Alejo and several vaqueros were busy running after hens and goats, while Campbell and two of his vaqueros cut the cabrito that had slowly roasted overnight on the fire of dry mesquite wood and others prepared hot sauce and fresh coffee.

Cheno enjoyed watching how the vaqueros skillfully tied the just caught goats and hens legs, putting them on a wagon, later to be taken to the main camp. This was the life he loved. The mist of the morning and the breeze caressing his body made him feel energized. As far as he was concerned, this could continue forever. He was so overwhelmed by the joy of the moment that he was about to join the roosters with a wild, happy crow, when suddenly sadness overcame him; he remembered that they were preparing for an upcoming showdown with the Army. Instead, he got up, chased and caught one of the running hens.

Afterward, they all gathered around the fire to enjoy a well- deserved breakfast.

"Cheno, I'm sorry to see you in this trouble," Campbell said as he handed a leg of the roasted goat to Cheno. "I, like the rest of people in the Valley, admire your courage and determination. Most of us, would have given up, even though fairness is on your side." He filled a cup of coffee and handed it to Chema who already had a piece of meat in a flour tortilla. "We prefer the easy way, just mind our own business and try to live in peace," he added.

"It's easy for people like you to say that. Nobody is trying to take away what is yours," Cheno replied.

"We are called bandoleros, rustlers," Alejo said juggling a hot tortilla he had just taken out of the stove.

"Be careful," Cheno said, laughing, "that tortilla is spirited, it might bite you." He stopped laughing before turning to face Campbell. "Alejo is right, they use the law to steal the land from its rightful owners, but because we try to prevent them, we are the bandoleros." He felt his cheeks turned red as he spoke. "They brand other's people cattle with their iron, but we are the rustlers because we get it back." His mouth felt dry and he took a sip of the bitter coffee, barely sweetened with cinnamon and brown sugar. He spat out part of the coffee. "We are being kicked out of our homes but we are the ones called plunderers." He opened his arms in helplessness, looked at Campbell, exhaled heavily and tried to smile.

"Soldiers are coming! The soldiers are coming!" an approaching vaquero yelled as he galloped towards them.

"Someone informed the soldiers that you are here," the vaquero told Cheno as soon as he got close. "They were getting ready to leave Brownsville when I left."

"We'd better go. Chema, Alejo, you be sure that the wagons and the men leave immediately" Cheno said before turning to Campbell, he extended his right hand to him. "Thank you for everything. I apologize for putting you through this. We'll send the payment for the hens and goats later."

Campbell smiled as he took Cheno's hand. "Don't worry about that. They claim that you are a rustler. Remember? I'll say that you stole it, and bill the army for it."

Cheno smiled back, extending his left arm to press Campbell's shoulder. "You are a good man and a good friend," he said. "Do as you please, we'll always remember your kindness." Chema and Alejo approached with Cheno's horse already saddled. He mounted, waived good bye and they galloped away.

Once they were at a safe distance, they stopped and Cheno climbed a tall oak tree. From there he observed the soldiers arriving at El Ebonal. He observed how the uniformed soldiers stayed on their horses while the rangers, like a wild bunch, dismounted and started chasing goats and hens. Cheno took his rifle and aimed at the commanding officer. He smiled and returned to his horse. They let the horses graze at leisure.

"Cheno, I'm glad you didn't fire," Chema said, soon afterwards.

"That would be too easy," Cheno replied. "Besides, I realize that if we start sniping, it will reinforce the myth that we are nothing but low class bandidos."

"It doesn't matter. For them that's exactly what we are," Alejo snapped. Cheno noticed a mixture of bitterness and sadness in his voice.

"What is truly important is how we feel about ourselves," Chema said. "As long as we keep it an honest fight, they may think whatever they want."

"That's the attitude, brother!" Cheno said, laughing as he slapped Chema's back. "We'll give them a hard fight, but it always be an honest and fair fight."

A noisy band of chachalacas suddenly ran in front of them. Behind the boisterous birds came a wild turkey, that was being chased by an ocelot, with a couple of graceful strides, the cat easily caught its prey.

Observing the scene, Cheno frowned, stopping his horse. "You two go ahead and move our camp to Rio Grande City. Almost everyone is friendly there," he said. "It will be easier to organize our defense."

"Where are you going?" Alejo asked.

"I'll go to El Carmen. I suddenly feel an urge to see Rafaela." His mouth was dry and a cold chill ran through his spine. "For some reason I'm afraid I'll never see her again."

"Go, brother," Chema said, extending his arm and touching Cheno's shoulder. "Go tranquil, we'll do as you said. And say hello to Rafaela and Mama." Alejo nodded agreeably.

"Thank you," Cheno said "I'll see you at Rio Grande City in a couple of days."

That night at El Carmen ranch, Cheno sat at the dinner table sharing the evening meal with Estefana, Rafaela and Sabas. Outside, the whistling sound of palm and tree leaves moved by the sea breeze and the humming of hundreds of birds and crickets provided a musical background. . Cheno wished he could stay outside listening to the relaxing sounds of nature, sounds that were so familiar and dear for him. Instead, he could feel the tension in Sabas facial expression and movements.

"Cheno," Sabas said. "Stop this nonsense and surrender to the authorities," Cheno sensed anger in his brother's voice. "You have no chances of winning and, in the process; you are putting all of us at risk." Sabas slammed the table making the dinnerware jump. Rafaela and Estefana jumped along with it. "Think, you idiot, think carefully what you are doing, because you are about to lose everything, but be sure that we'll not go down with you. We do not support you! Understand? We'll not go down with you!"

"Perhaps you haven't realized it," Cheno replied, feeling the blood rushing to his face. "But this fight is also for our own protection."

"How is that?" Sabas asked. "We have kept our property. We are respected and nobody has bothered us."

"Is that so?" Cheno snapped back. "Have you not seen our old friends and neighbors expelled from their own homes? Have you not been aware that their cattle has been rustled and branded? Have they not been accused and indicted as common robbers when they tried to get their property back? Tomas was assassinated. Are you blind?"

"Tomas was a member of the resistance. He brought disgrace to himself. Those who lost their land are a weak bunch of fools. And so are you. Do you think that you can wage a war against the United States and win it?"

"You well know that we aren't at war against United States. I, like most of the men fighting with me, accept the fact that we are now Americans. But that is exactly the matter. There are many who won't accept us as such. They would like us, all of those who were here before the war, to be wiped away. They claim to have conquered us." Cheno took a deep breath. "They expected that all of us would be like you; as

113

long as you keep your bone to chew you are a happy dog."

"Don't call me a dog!" Sabas yelled, snapping the table again and standing up.

Cheno also stood up. Eyes sparkling, muscles tense, jaw tight.

"Sons!" Estefana yelled, also standing up. "I don't want fighting at my home, both of you sit back down!"

"Cheno, your brother is right; you have no hope of winning. You are risking not only losing the fight but also your property and even your family. Rafaela is with child, your child, who you might never get to see. Yes, there is injustice and things aren't fair for everyone, but they have the law on their side. Since you are aware that you have no chances of winning; then, what is it that you are fighting for?"

"For pride and dignity, mother," Cheno whispered after a moment of thought. "For pride and dignity," he repeated in a louder voice. "We can't just stand aside while our old friends and neighbors are losing everything simply because they can't afford a shrewd lawyer. In reality the law is on our side, but they have bent it. We must restore our self respect. They have spread lies about us. If I surrender now it will mean that I admit that I'm the rustler, the bandolero as they have portrayed me."

"But son, you are risking so much. You will lose everything. What are you getting in exchange?" Estefana said.

"I've answered that, Mother. Pride and dignity. If I don't do it, I won't be able to look you, my wife or my child in the eyes," Cheno answered. "I would feel ashamed of myself."

"I think I understand you, son," Estefana said extending her arm to touch Cheno's hand tenderly. "I pray God to give you wisdom and guide you." She turned to look at Sabas and Rafaela. "We'll do everything within our power to keep the land for Rafaela. May God bless you son." She took Cheno's hand and kissed it.

"You are a fool, brother," Sabas said. "If we can't convince you to give up your reckless attitude, I agree with Mama. We'll do everything to keep the property for Rafaela and your child."

"Thank you, brother. I don't ask for anything else," Cheno said standing up and opening his arms to embrace Sabas who had stood up and returned his hug.

Later, once Cheno and Rafaela were alone in their bedroom, Cheno asked her. "Rafaela, what do you think? Should I just surrender and get this over with?"

"Cheno, you already answered that," Rafaela replied. "If you don't stand up for what you believe is right, you will be unhappy with yourself. I can see you feeling ashamed, making your life and everyone else around you, bitter." She stared at him, her black eyes sparkling. "No, I don't want that for you or for myself. I love you too much," she added throwing herself in Cheno's arms. "Hold me tight, hold me tight, please," she sobbed.

A few days later, at Rio Grande City, one hundred miles west of Brownsville, Chema, Cheno and Alejo rode through town together.

"People here are friendly, as you said they would be," Chema said. "But they are also scared." He pointed to the closed doors and windows. "The rangers have done a thorough job of putting fear in them."

"We have extended our defense to the edge of the river, that way we won't be attacked through that side and at same time, it will provide us with an escape route" Alejo said. "I hope the later won't be necessary," he added.

"I've been informed that the army and the rangers left Brownsville two days ago, which means they will arrive here tonight," Cheno said. "We'll put the cannons in the cemetery." He pointed to the promontory where the town cemetery was. "That will be our stronghold. Get the men ready. We should expect them to attack at dawn."

At dawn, the sharp sound of the bugle's fanfare, calling the army to battle, got both sides ready. It was a hot and humid morning; mosquitoes buzzing everywhere, the chirping of birds provided a pleasant background to the sound of the bugle. The bright sunrise colors illuminated the river, the town, the battlefield. Doves, sensing the imminent danger, flew away.

Cheno observed how the Army was getting ready to attack at his center. The rangers would come at his flanks. He frowned as bitter memories came to him when he saw the mobile cannons getting ready to attack.

"The weight of their assault will be on our center," Cheno told Alejo and Chema. "Their weakness is on their left side. If we can hold them on our center, we'll have a chance to break through their weak side and surround them. That will be our chance of winning."

"I'll put the Irish on charge of our cannons to fire on that side," Alejo said, slapping his cheek to kill a mosquito.

The army's artillery opened fire toward the cemetery. They were painfully accurate. Immediately after, their infantry charged. As Cheno was expecting, the rangers on horseback attacked his left side. The Irish, in charge of the cannons waited before shooting. This time they were accurate. That, and the rifle men on the trenches, stopped the rangers, forcing them to retreat. Meanwhile the men on the center were able to hold back the army's attack.

"This is our chance!" Cheno yelled. He let the reins of his horse free, riding ahead of forty mounted men. They caught up with the retreating rangers. A savage, bloody battle started, resulting in bodies cut by knives, sabers, machetes. Men and horses wounded by gunshot at short range. The rangers retreated.

Cheno, with a bloody machete in hand, felt close to accomplishing his plan. He was about to yell orders to pursue the retreating rangers, when he saw the army's cavalry galloping toward them, to reinforce the rangers. Cheno turned and noticed that his center had given up. They were about to be surrounded; if that happened, his route of escape would be closed.

"Retreat!" he yelled. "To the river, Chema let's get the cannons!"

Cheno, Chema and two other vaqueros galloped toward the cannons. Chema threw a lasso to one of the cannons, while one the vaqueros did the same to the other. All pulled at the cannons, but they were stuck.

"Forget it!" Cheno yelled to them. "Let's be sure that the retreat is orderly"

By that time everyone was running toward the river. Cheno, Chema, Alejo and some men other tried to make those running to turn and face the enemy, so they could retreat with some order, but it was to no avail. It was a human stampede.

Cheno feeling angered, turned his horse to face the oncoming soldiers.

"Cheno let's go!" Chema yelled. "We are defeated. But we still can get the men organized on the other side of the river."

Cheno turned to face Chema. His face felt flushed, his muscles tense, his body ready to continue the fight.

"Cheno!" Alejo yelled getting close and holding the reins of Cheno's horse. "There is no reason to die here, or worse to be captured. Let's go"

Cheno stared at Alejo, and then looked at the approaching soldiers.

"You are right," he said turning his horse.

They darted away. While crossing the river, Cheno noticed the struggle of many of his friends, although they had chosen a shallow area, the river was still turbulent and dangerous for those crossing on foot. Cheno saw how some men were wiped away by the treacherous undercurrent, hopelessness overcame him, and with a strong movement of his right hand he wiped the tears flowing freely down his cheeks. .

Later that night. Cheno, Chema, Alejo and their remaining followers got together few miles south of the border.

"At least sixty men are dead," Alejo said. "Some of them drowned while trying to cross the river.

"That's in addition to those who were captured and those who have deserted us," Chema said. "It has been a crushing defeat."

Cheno sat, pensive. "Yes, we have been defeated, this time," he said. "But, we'll continue fighting."

"Cheno, remember that the conservatives in Matamoros are also against us," Alejo said.

"We have become a nuisance for business on both sides of the border," Chema said. "We can count on support from the people, but most of the wealthy merchants are all against us."

Chema got up and threw a log into the fire.

"We aren't asking for much," Cheno said. "Just to be allowed to keep what has been ours for a long time. To have the treaty respected. We still have a chance of being listened. We'll go to La Bolsa. Once there we'll plan what to do next."

"It seems to me that you are not listening brother," Chema said. "The wealthy merchants on both sides want us to be defeated. It's no longer a matter of fairness. We are preventing them from making money. They have convinced everyone in Texas that we are nothing but common bandits." Upset he threw another log onto the fire.

"But we are not bandits," Alejo said. "We didn't provoke this struggle. We are only defending our rights."

"We must be conscious of the circumstances," Chema said. "Indeed, our cause is just. The common folks see it that way, but once again; those against us have convinced everyone else of the contrary. Today's defeat shows that the authorities in Austin won't listen to us. The conservatives in power in Matamoros support the idea of secession by the southern states. At the same time, they need the support of the Texas authorities. The central government in Mexico is too weak and won't care about our struggle."

"You worry about too many things brother," Cheno said.

"We must be realistic, Cheno," Chema replied.

"What about them?" Cheno asked pointing to the more than one hundred men tending their wounds. "Shouldn't we also listen to them?"

"But, Cheno, if we already know the result of it. What will any of us gain?"

"Probably not much in the eyes of some, but much on our own: Pride and dignity," Cheno answered. "That's not small matter. We can't just stand aside."

"I understand you, brother," Chema said, standing up and walking towards Cheno. "But this time I can't follow you. I'll go and fight in a different way. It may take longer, but I believe that, under the circumstances, it's the only reasonable way."

Wearily Cheno pushed up off the ground, walked to Chema and hugged him. "May God bless you." He then turned to face the rest of the men. "Anyone who wishes to leave, feel free to go," he yelled.

"We'll stay," the Comanche chief replied.

Most of the men came to their feet. "We'll also stay," one of the Irish men spoke for the group.

A couple of days later at La Bolsa, so called because it was a place where the river bent in such a way that a small peninsula was created. Cheno had chosen the place because he knew that the only way to approach it was from the Mexican side of the river.

117

Cranes and storks fished in the river, hundreds of seagulls flew overhead while wild ducks and peacocks walked on the riverbank. Years before Tomas had taken Cheno and his brothers to this place for hunting and fishing. Pleasant memories came to Cheno's mind as they prepared to camp.

Lorenzo Garza, who had come from Matamoros along with Felix Cortez, approached him and said. "Cheno there are rumors that Kenedy's steamboat, El Ranchero will be carrying a cargo worth a quarter of a million dollars. From here it would easy for you to attack and get it. That money would help you to finance the struggle."

"That might be true, but we are not common bandoleros," Cheno answered. "Until now I've told my men that we must respect others' property. We'll not start stealing now."

"You are being naïve," Lorenzo said.

"We are not naïve, just honest," Alejo snapped, standing up and kicking a stone that flew and accidentally hit a toad.

"You must be careful," Lorenzo said. "Unfortunately, things have got much worse for the peasants in both sides of the border. The rangers attack indiscriminately causing fear in the people." He took off his broad-brimmed hat, and wiped the sweat from his forehead. "They blame you for every misdeed that happens in the valley."

"Maybe we are just chasing the smoke," Cheno said. "Perhaps it's time for us to give up."

"No, what you are doing is courageous. You and these valiant men have stood up for all of us. You have made us proud," Lorenzo replied. "Folks are singing corridos dedicated to you in every cantina in town." He paused for a moment, pensive. "Most of us are cowards. We see the problem, but we prefer to mind first about our own business and we look the other way. It's sad but that's the way it is." He paused. "Watch out. The rangers might use the cargo on El Ranchero as an excuse to attack you."

"We are safe here," Alejo said. "We are on the Mexican side, and because the current in the river here slows down the water is deep and treacherous, so the only way to attack us is through this side."

"Cheno," Felix Cortez, said, "I also admire your courage; but as Lorenzo says, I also care about my own business and in this case, my business is my daughter, Rafaela." He sighed, paused for a moment; he looked like he was searching for words. "You are a good man and I know you love Rafaela and she loves you," he continued. "But, I also know that you are a dreamer; if it's not this fight, there will be another, you'll never stop fighting. That's the way you are," he looked around still searching for words. "I don't want that for my daughter, if you go back home you will endanger her and your entire family. You shouldn't go back."

Cheno looked at him, feeling a deep pain in his chest, he still attempted to smile. "I'll never endanger her," he said.

When night came, it was unusually dark, the moon and the stars hided behind heavy clouds. The crickets and toads sang their ritual song, when, suddenly, they became silent. Cheno slept soundly and in his dream, he was fishing along with Rafaela and a little girl, their daughter. Tomas was cooking the just caught fish. At that moment he was aroused by one of the Comanche.

"Horses are approaching," the Comanche said.

"Get the men ready," Cheno ordered, getting up and going for his rifle and gun. "Saddle the horses. We might have to get out of here in a hurry."

Suddenly bullets came. Wild, primitive, violent screams were heard. They were being attacked from the south bank.

Cheno and Alejo tried to get the men organized but the continuous gunfire coming from the only entrance to the small peninsula, prevented them from any form of resistance. They couldn't retreat, the only way out was going through the enemy's line.

Cheno, Alejo, the Comanche and all of the others gathered together and let the reins of their horses free as they charged courageously against the invisible enemy. The returning fire was fierce. Riding in the dark, Cheno could feel and hear men falling. He kept on galloping and firing until he could sense that they had crossed the enemy's line. At that moment, the clouds allowed the moon to shine.

On reaching a promontory, Cheno turned his horse and saw El Ranchero boat beyond the bend of the river. A bullet struck the cantle of his saddle. Across the river was the land of his childhood and youth, the land that he loved dearly. He realized that he wouldn't be allowed to go back. A second bullet pulled his hat away taking with it a lock of hair. There, in the distance, Cheno could image Rafaela, carrying his child; it felt well to know that she was sheltered.

A third bullet cut his bridle rein. Would he ever see her again? Would they share happy moments again? A fourth bullet passed through his horse's ear and the animal neighed and flinched in pain. Using only the strength of his legs, Cheno controlled his horse. Would he ever know his child? A fifth bullet struck his belt. I hope it's a girl, Cheno thought, as beautiful as her mother. He realized that this struggle was lost. There was no sense on keeping on this path. If he continued he would have to become a bandolero, as they already were calling him.

He felt pain at the thought of all that had been lost. He had lost not only the struggle, but also his land, his money and his family. The people that he had tried to defend were treated worse than before. It was a total defeat. For pride and dignity, he thought, at least I have that; and for now, that's enough. Dark clouds covered the moon, heavy tear drops fell. Feeling refreshed, Cheno lifted his head letting the rain drops wash away his tears. Thunderbolts illuminated the sky. Cheno put his horse on two legs, raising his right hand he waived farewell and turning his horse, he galloped away. Alejo, the Comanche, and those still loyal, followed him.